A Chorus of Seven

A Collection of Short Stories and Poems

By

The Scriveners

Quantum Dot Press
2020

First Published 2020 by Quantum Dot Press

www.quantumdotpress.com

ISBN: 978-1-912882-29-8

Andrew Burns
Vindolanda 1; Vindolanda 2; Evestone Lake; A Love Story; Mick Campbell and Murphy's Law; Heaven Helps...; Peter Comes to Stay

Sue I'Anson
It wouldn't be Christmas without...; Memory; A day in my life; I must go down to the sea...; Sunday - Past Senses; Rulers of the deep; A stroke of Luck; United?

Judith Lonsdale
Street Portrait, 1950; Norfolk Watercolour; Bereft; About Water; Seventeen Seagulls: A Norse Skyline; A Late Summer Lunch; The Walled Garden

Marla Skidmore
The Stripper; Elegy; Battlefield Tour; Ruined; Waiting for Papa; A Hint of History; Military Manoeuvres

Kathleen Swann
Adrift; City Dwellers; Song of the Tide on Walney Island; Corvus Girl; Piel Island in the Wind; Wide-Eyed; Turpentine & Beeswax

Lesley Taylor
Roses and Grapes; The Busker; Desert Water; Georgie Goes Missing; Long green skirts; Old hands; Old Love

Sue Williams
Molly's Story; True Lust; Putting the Record Straight - a story about the Brontes; Return to Pemberley; Second Best; Cosily Confidential; Patrick's Return

Cover design by Edwin Rydberg
www.lightspeeddreams.net

A Chorus of Seven

A Collection of Short Stories and Poems

By

The Scriveners

Table of Contents

Introduction to A Chorus of Seven   VIII

ANDREW BURNS   1

Vindolanda 1   2
Vindolanda 2   3
Evestone Lake   4
A Love Story   5
Mick Campbell and Murphy's Law   6
Heaven Helps...   10
Peter Comes to Stay   17

SUE I'ANSON   33

It wouldn't be Christmas without...   34
Memory   35
A day in my life   36
Sunday – Past senses   38
I must go down to the sea.......   40
Rulers of the deep   41
A stroke of luck   42
United?   43

JUDITH LONSDALE   45

Street Portrait, 1950   46
Norfolk Watercolour   48
Bereft   49
About Water   50
Seventeen Seagulls: A Norse Skyline   51
A Late Summer Lunch   52
The Walled Garden   57

MARLA SKIDMORE   63

The Stripper   64
Elegy   65
Battlefield Tour   66
Ruined   67
Waiting for Papa   68
A Hint of History   72
Military Manoeuvres   77

KATHLEEN SWANN   85

Adrift   86
City Dwellers   87
Song of the Tide on Walney Island   88
Corvus Girl   89
Piel Island in the Wind   90
Wide-Eyed   91
Turpentine & Beeswax   92

LESLEY TAYLOR   95

Roses and grapes   96
The Busker   97
Desert Water   98
Georgie Goes Missing   101
Long green skirts   105
Old hands   106
Old Love   107

Molly's Story 112
True Lust 118
Putting the Record Straight – a story about the Brontes 119
Return to Pemberley 123
Second Best 128
Cosily Confidential 134
Patrick's Return 136

Acknowledgements

The Scriveners acknowledge the support of Ripon & District U3A and thank The Old Deanery for making them so welcome.

Introduction to A Chorus of Seven

Writers are like clouds; they float above and through life, absorbing fragments of location, relationships and emotion. This dialogue of humanity and existence is unconsciously stored until the time comes to indulge in an irresistible craving to convert a collection of thoughts into words on a page. Time may delay this process, but nothing can suppress it.

In May 2013 a creative writing group was established. It was based in one of the smallest and most charming Cathedral cities in North Yorkshire. Its opening was part of a new branch of the U3A, founded locally the previous year. Most of the members of the group barely knew each other; some were complete 'incomers'. It was a great starting point.

From those early days the group has grown into a settled circle of passionate writers who feel able to present widely differing writing styles to each other, confident of honest, constructive feedback and unwavering support. Shallow praise has no place in the critique practice or with fiendish proofreaders. The members feel comfortable with each other, both as friends and emerging writers.

From the ease of knowing each other well, comes the confidence and courage to experiment with different voices. Some members started the group with work already published some had not; some had been invited to include work in greater anthologies, or popular publications, others had serious work in progress. Since then, more published works have been added to the general list. These include an anthology of poetry, a work of historical fiction, a collection of writing and a well-received handbook for social care.

The progress of these recent publications – every faltering step and final success – has been followed and felt by each writer and is at least partially responsible for the slim volume you hold in your hand. It was clearly time for the group to go to 'Print'.

While *A Chorus of Seven* is rooted in the ancient charms of a Cathedral city, each of its writers springs from a different background. It is that collective contrast of childhood, careers, locations and livelihood, relationships, travel and humanity which formulates every piece of writing, but it is style and talent which enrich each voice. This collection of poetry and short stories explores observations of nature, loves lost and found, mischievous portraits, sadness and joy, reflections and challenges of contemporary life and past times.

The writers are: Andrew Burns, Sue I'Anson, Judith Lonsdale, Marla Skidmore, Kate Swann, Lesley Taylor and Sue Williams. You will find more about each one of them in their personal sections in the collection. After considering many different names for the group it was settled as *The Scriveners*, meeting regularly, as befits the title, in the atmospheric and historic Old Deanery, in the shadow of the Cathedral.

Here is the collection, told in seven voices, which is recommended for your generous appraisal, utter satisfaction and delight.

*The Scriveners present: **A Chorus of Seven***

Andrew Burns

Andrew Burns spent his working life in Derbyshire as a primary schools' teacher and adviser. He was a village school headteacher in the Peak District for fourteen years

Throughout his career he had written fiction and non-fiction material for schools and often wrote with the children in his class.

In retirement in North Yorkshire Andrew has written for his own pleasure and, as a member of a writer's group, hopefully for the enjoyment of others.

He mostly writes somewhat quirky short stories, Haiku and has completed an as yet unpublished novel.

***Vindolanda** is an exciting Northumbrian Roman site at Hadrian's Wall where an extensive archaeological project has been running for many years.*

Vindolanda 1

Roman life exposed
digging in morning sunlight
soon exhibits found

lives in layered soil
earth softens in spring sunlight
letters home appear

These Haiku are part of a series inspired by sitting quietly at the site in several locations over several hours.

Vindolanda 2

lone white daffodil
stands in a sea of yellow
facing the spring sun

green mist of buds
lyre shaped conifer branches
freshly filtered air

white noise rushing stream
echoing birds shrill singing
plaintive curlee curlee

energising sun
emerging Roman relics
silence peace and calm

These Haiku are part of a series that were written on visiting the lake for the first time. The lake is well hidden from any major road and had a unique, peaceful atmosphere.

Evestone Lake

bird songs echoes
tall trees lean in dappled light
Swans dip in still lake

huge gritstone outcrops
loom over secret valley
silent calm waters

ancient fallen logs
dry leaves among fresh bluebells
sound of tree felling

swans drift on still lake
parents watch for intruders
cygnets safe for now

light flickers above
fresh green leaves glow in sunlight
dry leaves under foot

This story was written in response to a challenge to a writing group to write a love story.

I decided that I would like to write something that related to the natural world in some way rather than to human relationships.

A Love Story

My mother always said that I should never have a relationship with a red head or a northerner.

I first met him while exploring a wood to the north of my usual neighbourhood. He rather crept up on me and I was somewhat startled! At first, I was annoyed at this intrusion but, after I calmed down somewhat, I was very taken by his beautiful bright eyes and gentle manner.

For a while we walked together in companionable silence and spent our time taking in the sights and smells of our leafy surroundings. Once we disturbed a grouse or a pheasant and were both alarmed by the sudden burst of noise they made crashing through the undergrowth!

The light began to fade but neither of us was in any mood to end the encounter. We strolled on together, deeper and deeper into the wood, loving the bosky light.

Neither of us could decide who actually made the first move but the move was most definitely made, and much enjoyed by both of us.

We parted, convinced we would meet again.

A couple of months later, I gave birth to four beautiful, bright red fox cubs.

Mick Campbell and Murphy's Law

Mick Campbell slowly emerged from under the duvet and proceeded to try and read the time on his alarm clock without his glasses.

08:38

He made a grab for his glasses and, putting them on, took a second look.

08:40

Staring around the unfamiliar hotel room, trying to get his bearings proved difficult as the thick curtains kept out any trace of daylight.

He leapt out of bed, knocking his clock onto the tiled floor. He stared in amazement at the surprisingly large number of clock parts that had scattered across the room.

Rushing into the *ensuite* bathroom, Mick discovered that the floor was flooded. He slipped in the slimy water causing him to crack his head on a cast iron radiator.

Nursing his sore head with a moistened hotel flannel, he struggled into his clothes. His shirt stuck to his wet back and his head bled into his collar, despite the flannel.

He realised two things simultaneously.

He was in need of a good English breakfast and he had to be somewhere else in town, very soon.

Locking his bedroom door and setting off down a long, brown-carpeted, corridor, he reached an external fire door. Retracing his steps, he followed the clear signs to the lift.

He pressed every button in sight at least three times, to no avail. Then he noticed the yellow plastic sign indicating that the lift was 'Under maintenance.'

He made for the stairs, and soon realised that there are an awful lot of steps when you start off from the tenth floor!

He arrived on the ground floor and, gasping for breath, set off towards the Breakfast Room. He was greeted by a member of staff in an immaculate white jacket.

"Sorry sir, we stop serving breakfast at 09.00."

Retracing his steps for the second time that morning, he climbed twenty short flights of stairs back to his room. He found a packet of stale Hobnobs on his complimentary drinks tray and stuffed them into his mouth between gasps for air.

Piling clothes and possessions into his overnight bag, he made for the door and set off towards the stairs again.

On the ground floor he discovered that other guests were leaving the newly serviced lift.

He queued at the reception desk for what seemed like hours. The clock on the wall was showing 09:14.

He reached the front of the queue to discover that it was solely for bookings for the fitness suite.

Reaching the front of the right queue at the correct desk, he found that he had left his cheque book at home and was forced to try his credit card. It was rejected due to "insufficient funds" being available.

A porter escorted him down the road to an ATM. His debit card was accepted, and the machine paid out half of the cash he had requested and promptly returned his card before closing down.

He followed the porter back to the hotel, put a ten-pound note into the outstretched hand and queued again to settle his account. It was now 09.40.

At last he could set off for his appointment.

Every black cab ignored him, even when he stood in the centre of the road. A bus just managed to stop in time, avoiding running him over by a whisker, with a very rude tirade from the driver. Mick got on, and off again. He had no change nor a travel card.

He got out the Google map he had been sent and walked off, in the wrong direction. An almost unintelligible traffic warden finally set him off on the correct route with a series of grunts, crazy hand signals and exasperated sighs.

Mick arrived at a vastly impressive ultramodern headquarters building. He went into reception and was approached by a uniformed security guard who demanded, politely and firmly, some sort of ID.

Mick found an expired Blockbuster Video membership card in an inside pocket and, seconds later, was standing outside on a crowded pavement.

Mick searched his jacket pockets, his hold-all, his pockets(again), his hold-all (ditto) and came across a letter about his appointment screwed up in a trouser pocket with some chewing gum and a rather rank handkerchief.

He re-entered the building and once again faced the guard. Mick handed him the letter that he then held at arm's length by one corner and led the way to the receptionist.

She smoothed out the letter and reached for some hand gel. She checked a long list of names on her computer screen.

"We've been expecting you since 09.00 this morning......sir."

Before he could respond, the receptionist pressed a button on her intercom and (loudly) announced that, "Mick Campbell is now in reception, would anyone from Desert Island Discs please come and collect him and take him to studio 3?"

Well, thought Mick, what could possibly go wrong now?

At that moment all the lights went out, the alarms sounded, and the sprinkler system was activated.

Heaven Helps…

It was mid-morning when I arrived in the small town after a very slow journey on a filthy, old and overcrowded two carriage train.

I was glad I hadn't wasted money on a ticket.

I walked from the station along quiet, tree-lined streets and made my way towards the high street and the modest branch of Marks and Spencer that I had looked up on Google the night before.

This was supposed to be my day off and, generally, I got away for a few hours visiting towns around the Midlands to do some basic shopping. It was so good to walk around a town without being recognised. In my hometown or neighbourhood it took me ages to get my shopping done because everyone seemed to have something they just had to tell me! Today was like heaven.

The town was not crowded, and I soon found the branch of Marks and Spencer, one I hadn't visited before.

It was rather cool for the time of year and I cursed myself for not bringing a coat with me.

I made my way towards the menswear department, found a light overcoat in my size and put it on. It was a perfect fit.

I selected a few shirts, a couple of ties and a week's supply of socks and underwear. Fortunately, I always carry a newish plastic M&S bag in my pocket. In no time at all, I had stuffed the clothes in the bag without attracting attention from the staff. I smiled to myself: this was looking like a good day.

I noticed that some new stock had arrived, silk dressing gowns. No, no, enough was enough for today and anyway, the bag was getting rather heavy.

Passing through the subterranean food hall, I decided against taking any food today as I fancied something hot in a pub.

The store was getting busy and I felt rather hot after my efforts, it was time to go. Without any sense of haste, I made my way up the escalator and ambled towards the main doors, only stopping occasionally to inspect furniture and kitchenware.

Outside in the nearby shopping arcade, I calmly stopped to do up my shoelace and spent some time looking at the window display in the Ann Summers store. I wandered along, looking at a variety of goods in the windows of the row of shops, enjoying the sights and smells of a new location.

At the end of the street, I decided that I was bored with shopping and recognised the return of my pangs of hunger. I decided to leave the town and go to a village pub for an early lunch. I needed a car. Not a problem, thanks to a specialist retailer of electronic gizmos on Amazon.

After a short walk, I saw a newish Mercedes convertible parked in a quiet side street on double yellow lines. Typical of that sort of owner to leave it in such a thoughtless manner. The locks on a Mercedes were dead easy to open if you know how and the alarm was not switched on. I had my new clever electronic device in my pocket and I just loved the quiet clunk of the car doors unlocking. I put my bag in the small boot, slung the new overcoat on the back seat and drove out of town onto the bypass, only then noticing that the fuel gauge was bleeping and flashing empty. How irritating. I pressed a second button on my piece of electronic wizardry, and the engine fired up with a very satisfactory deep roar.

There was a garage up ahead and I pulled up to a pump. The car seemed to take a vast amount of fuel and the prices were considerably higher than I was used to. I closed the fuel cap, got back behind the wheel and drove off at some speed and took a left turn onto the inner ring road. I could only snigger at the thought of the actual owner getting a visit from the police.

The car was soon up to 95 mph, and with the hood down, I was really enjoying myself. Too late, I spotted the Day-Glo jacketed

Police Officer with the radar gun. I decided there was no time to ease up, so I flashed past him at just over 80. Within seconds, I heard the wail of a police car siren, this was going to be fun. The police van did not stand a chance of catching me and I smiled as I watched it getting smaller in the rear-view mirror. and I was pleased to be able to carve up a line of cars crawling behind two heavy lorries, leaving a lot of road and much traffic between the law and myself.

For the rest of the morning, I drove more slowly along winding, peaceful country lanes, listening to Radio Three. I arrived at a pub I had read about in the Sunday Times. It had been given five stars for the lunch menu, despite the exorbitant prices. The pub car park was empty except for a new, top of the range Land Rover Discovery. I parked next to it.

In the bar, the publican was leaning on the pumps reading the Financial Times. I looked at the lunch time menu and ordered the priciest starter of the day, a medium rare steak to follow, despite the outrageous five-pound surcharge, and to finish, with a disgustingly creamy pudding for an eye-watering £7.00. A bottle of reasonable red wine costing a further £15.00 kept me going through the excellent meal.

I sat at a small table facing the door. Always a wise precaution, I found. I looked around the bar but recognised no one among the few lunch time customers. I tend to eat rather quickly when alone, so in less than twenty-five minutes I headed for the gents, and in seconds, I was out through the tiny toilet window and back out in the car park, breaking into the Discovery. It seemed like a fair swap for the Mercedes which was rather too well known to the police now.

My car breaking gadget worked a great and in no time at all, with the front windows open and the stereo playing 'Wagner' at full volume, I headed towards another large town sprawling below me in a smoky valley.

I stopped in a lay-by and searched through the glove compartment of the Discovery. (You'd be amazed how stupid people are about leaving valuables in their car.)

Right at the back, was a small wallet containing two credit cards together with a membership card for a casino in this very town and a very expensive mobile phone! Some people are just so trusting and predictable. I pocketed the wallet and phone, thinking of the joy they might bring to the rest my day off.

I drove the Discovery to the end of a lay-by, out of sight from the road behind a block of pine trees. Within seconds, the interior was ablaze and as I walked towards the main road, I heard the whoosh of the petrol tank exploding.

A few yards down the road, I turned on my newly acquired phone and called a cab. I lobbed the phone into a corn field, stood at the roadside and watched the emergency services rushing towards the lay-by and the burning vehicle. As I watched, I did not hear the cab arrive and the driver made me jump when he called out my (assumed) name from the window of his rather battered Granada. I asked for the station.

We crawled along in very heavy traffic. The driver wanted to talk about his favourite football team. I merely grunted in reply and he soon got the message that I was not a chatty customer. I got him to drop me off by the rear exit of the station, saying that I would be right back when I had found out the time of my train. I walked straight through the booking hall, out of the front entrance and made for a bank.

Some banks are getting very keen on security, but I risked asking for five hundred pounds on the credit card. The young cashier was very rushed and barely looked at the card or my signature. When I got outside, I was delighted to see that he had given me fifty pounds too much!

I hailed another cab and gave the name of the casino. This time, I paid off the cab with some dodgy bank notes that I'd acquired in Birmingham on my trip a week ago.

Inside the casino, I left my coat and my shopping bag with the cloakroom attendant, ordered a large brandy and set to work on the vulgar, flashing machines. I was in my element and soon doubled my money using another clever bit of electronic wizardry that I had bought from a very dodgy site on the internet.

I didn't want to attract too much attention, so I moved from machine to machine and took care to lose money from time to time. I soon got bored and retrieved my 'magic' black box from under the noisy, flashing, electronic machine, collected my coat and bag and sauntered towards the door.

"Sir!"

I kept walking but felt a hand on my arm.

I turned to face the inevitable trouble. A young waiter let go of my arm, somewhat embarrassed.

"Sir, I hope you don't mind me mentioning it...." "What do you want with me?" I snapped.

"Excuse me, sir", persisted the waiter, "but you still have the shop label on your coat. Would you like me to cut it off for you?"

"That is most kind, young man, thank you". I sounded a lot calmer than I felt. I sent him away with a twenty-pound note in his hand (a real one, I must be losing my touch).

I left the casino and decided not to risk another cab. I managed to catch a bus back into the town centre, and even avoided paying my fare!

I walked to a different bank and put my winnings into my number two account. You can't walk around carrying that sort of money – there are so many crooks around!

I needed a car, so I headed back to the railway station. There were no cabs parked outside, I was pleased to note.

I went to the car hire office; the choice of vehicles was quite daunting. I settled for a modest Jaguar and paid in full on the credit card I had found in the Discovery. I told the clerk that I would be leaving the car at their branch in Manchester the next day. I was rather late, so wasted no time in getting onto the urban motorway and then joined the M6. The Jag was quite a machine, and, after a thrilling few miles, I eased back from 130 miles per hour to a more sedate 90.

I was back in Birmingham with about half an hour to spare. I drove very slowly along the Bristol Road, and turned into a narrow driveway between a pub and a Quaker Meeting House. At the rear of the pub was a row of lock up garages. I knocked lightly on the rusty doors of the end unit.

I left the Jag with a 'friend' who could have it out of the country in less than 24 hours, having settled for two thousand pounds for a car worth at least twenty thousand. I really must be getting soft these days.

Time was definitely not on my side. Back on the Bristol Road I hailed a bus, showed my pass and sat behind the driver. I had to get home, hang up my new clothes and get changed for work.

I ran home from the bus stop, avoiding two elderly ladies who obviously had something they just had to tell me there and then. I changed quickly. I got out my old bike and peddled off down the road, waving greetings to even more old ladies who all wanted to stop for a chat. "Sorry, must rush, see you tomorrow!" I shouted.

I arrived with seconds to spare, threw the bike behind a pile of dead leaves and let myself in by a small side door. I was only just in time, as I walked in a blast of very loud music warned me that I had work to do.

"Dearly beloved we are gathered here today to witness the marriage of Tracey and Kevin…"

*   *   *

"Thank you so much Vicar, a lovely wedding. So much better when it's taken by a man as spiritual as you are."

"Thank you for your kind comments, I only do my humble best. Goodbye."

I walked away from them as they threw confetti at the church door. I had the best man's wallet in my cassock pocket and whistled as I left the wedding party, retrieved my bike and made my way back towards to my rather scruffy study in my draughty Victorian vicarage.

"I'm home!" I made a grab for the study door handle, but my elderly mother stood in my way.

She said, "Hello love, come into the lounge, there's someone here who wants a word with you. Quite a few words in fact".

For a moment I froze. Was it time to run?

I decided it would be better to face the music. I opened the lounge door and went in.

Peter Comes to Stay

Marjorie Mycock and husband George were delighted that their teenage nephew, Peter, was coming to stay on their rather remote Peak District farm. Marjorie told Ben Peterson, the postman, about the newcomer who was soon to arrive on the farm.

"George and I are, well, let's just say we'll never see seventy again and we're a little daunted at the prospect of an autistic teenager coming to stay for an extended holiday."

Peter had not visited the hill farm very often, but it was decided that his parents needed a break from him, and he probably needed a break from them. His mother, Grace, was Marjorie's younger sister and her husband was Henry, George's younger brother. They were real townies and lived in a terraced house in Salford, near Manchester. This was a total contrast to the ancient farm high in the bleak hills of the Derbyshire Peak District.

Grace always claimed to suffer 'with her nerves' and they had Peter rather late in life. By the time he was ready to start primary school, they were disconcerted by what they considered to be his increasingly very strange behaviour. They had tried to ignore this in the hope that he would grow out of it once he started school.

Sadly, soon after his first few weeks in his large urban primary school, he was described by one teacher after another as 'unteachable' and the Headteacher, Gail Griffiths, called Henry and Grace into school to discuss their son's future.

In a rather irritable meeting, she suggested that it was vital he was sent to see an Educational Psychologist as soon as possible.

After an inconclusive appointment with the Ed.Psych, there followed many consultations with a variety of child experts.

Eventually, it was decided that Peter was a high-functioning autistic boy and needed to transfer elsewhere, as the school was not geared up to teach children with his condition.

Another discussion was arranged with a senior Area Education Officer who told Peter's parents that the local authority had nothing to offer their son in this area. He explained that the LEA was prepared to fund a place for Peter in a specialist boarding school in rural North Yorkshire.

Henry and Grace were delighted that someone was able to suggest a way forward for their son. Without a second thought, they agreed to take up a place for Peter at the boarding school. Peter wasn't given much of a say in the matter.

After a couple weeks waiting for his place to be confirmed, they quickly packed Peter's clothes and belongings in a large trunk and drove him to the school. They unceremoniously left him with the Head and set off back to Salford, convinced that this was for the best for Peter.

The school was housed in a slightly scruffy country mansion, with extensive grounds and an excellent staff to pupil ratio that was rated as 'the best provision for autistic boys in the north'.

Sadly, Peter hated everything about the school. He was terrified of the dark, the sounds of the wind in the trees that surrounded the school, every other pupil and most of the members of staff. He also made it very clear that he loathed the food.

He especially disliked the fact that, as a younger pupil, he had to sleep in a small three bed dormitory, and not in a room of his own. He actually stayed, rather grumpily, at the school for two years but never really settled.

The staff of the school were highly committed to all of the boys' education and wellbeing, but they were somewhat defeated by Peter, much to their deep regret.

Things came to a crisis point, when he was in his early teens. He ran away three times in a couple of weeks, trying to make his way home to Salford. Each time, he was returned in a police car during the night. With great sadness, the Head asked Henry and Grace to take him away from the school on a permanent basis.

After a year at home with a variety of tutors, who all failed completely to establish any sort of rapport with Peter, his parents asked Grace's extended family for help. That's how it came about that George was parked in the car park outside Matlock Station, waiting for Peter to arrive by train with his father.

George climbed out of his battered Range Rover as soon as he heard the train approaching the peaceful terminus.

The dirty, diesel train had clattered noisily into the station and screeched to a halt. Peter and his dad were the only passengers who got off, spotting George standing by the footbridge.

To George's amazement, Henry greeted him gruffly, put down Peter's suitcase, shook his son's hand and turned back towards the train and climbed into the rear carriage. Almost immediately, the driver revved up the engines noisily, the horn hooted discordantly and the train proceeded to clatter back down the line towards Derby, in a pother of diesel fumes.

Peter and George stood in silence, watching the train as it passed under a rusting bridge and, taking a slight turn to the left, rattled out of sight. Soon, they were standing all alone on the platform in total silence.

"Well, Peter, Marjorie and I are really happy that you're here to stay with us on our farm. We're about to start haymaking, there are a few calves that you might like to feed, and the sheep to keep an eye on too."

None of this made much sense to Peter so he said nothing, but glumly handed over his suitcase and climbed into the battered vehicle.

He didn't say a word to George on the way home but stared intently out of the mud-splattered side window. As they drove towards the farm, the view changed from tree-lined lanes to bleak-looking moorland, with dry stone walls enclosing a scattering of sheep grazing on rough grassland.

George drove into a rutted farmyard and parked outside a farmhouse that looked to Peter as though it had grown out of the surrounding landscape.

Marjorie was pleased to see Peter and almost immediately took him up to his bedroom. It had a low ceiling as it was high up, under the stone-tiled roof.

Peter looked around cautiously but didn't miss seeing the new-looking laptop computer and printer, on a large oak desk under the window. Neither did he miss the broadband router on the windowsill. He smiled nervously and asked if he could spend some time alone in his room. Having pointed out where the bathroom was, just down the corridor, Marjorie left the lad to settle in.

As soon as she left him, Peter emptied his suitcase and laid everything out neatly on the spare single bed. He arranged his six shirts in the order he would wear them and his three pairs of spare trousers in a complicated arrangement of his own devising.

He discovered empty drawers in an ancient-looking wardrobe and put away his socks and underwear according to a particular system that had taken him a long time to devise at his hated boarding school.

He was taken aback to notice that he felt more relaxed and peaceful than he could remember, in fact, he felt happy to be with Marjorie and George. Generally speaking, he was indifferent to adults and very wary of making new relationships.

Eventually, Peter went downstairs to the huge, low-beamed old-fashioned kitchen. A rather scruffy Aga cooker made the room exceedingly hot and there was an overpowering smell of fresh bread. Two loaves sat cooling on wire racks on the scrubbed pine table.

Glen, the sheepdog was asleep, almost too close to the very hot Aga. He looked up when Peter came into the room, and then went back to his dreams.

This was all quite out of Peter's experience, and he was unnerved to feel completely comfortable in this ancient building, with these gentle people.

George was sitting at one end of the table reading a thick farming magazine.

Marjorie was standing at the Aga, cooking a large pan of vegetables on the hot plate and had just taken a thick crusted pie out of the warming oven.

They both greeted Peter in their quiet manner and invited him to sit at the table next to George. Peter loved the heavy pine chairs and the thick sea.

Peter was surprised to discover that he was ravenous! He didn't have to be told twice to tuck into his steaming plate of vegetables and a large slice of meat pie, covered in a thick gravy. He was even more taken aback when he agreed to have another slice of the pie, liberally covered in the aromatic gravy.

George and Marjorie smiled across the table at each other. This was a boy that they had been told was very difficult to get on with, extremely fussy about the food he would eat, and yet here he was, in their kitchen, tucking into a classic farmhouse meal.

Marjorie put a large bowl of fresh fruit on the table and Peter managed to find room for the biggest banana for his pudding.

After their lunch, George offered to show Peter around the farm.

They left the warmth of the kitchen and walked across the yard to where George proudly pointed out his award-winning gritstone ewes in a small paddock, and then stopped to admire his impressive male tup in a pen on his own in the barn. Glen followed them everywhere.

Peter wasn't quite over his fear of dogs (an issue for him from a very early age). He was prepared to concede that Glen seemed friendly enough.

Later that day, in another big shed, Peter watched as George and Marjorie worked together in harmony getting in the Friesian cows, cleaning their udders and attaching the milking machine to their teats. This made gentle pumping sounds as the milk spurted into a line of large glass vessels.

George turned a tap when the last cow left the milking parlour, and the milk drained into the large stainless-steel tank in the next building. They both then set to hosing out the parlour until it was spotlessly clean.

Peter peered into the large milk tank and watched the paddles swishing around keeping the milk from separating from the cream. It was cooling the milk very quickly.

George took some of the fresh milk into a small shed and showed Peter how to bottle-feed the dozen young calves that seemed pleased to see him. They all drank the fresh, warm milk with great enthusiasm.

Peter noticed that one of the calves was very reluctant to feed, appearing very shaky on its legs.

He pointed this out to George, who put the calf in a smaller pen on its own. He was privately very impressed by Peter's observation skills.

Just before teatime, a tanker arrived from the Hartington Creamery and pumped the milk from the tank. The driver gave George a ticket stating how much he was taking away that time.

Peter watched the whole process, quite fascinated by what happened to the milk. After a brief conversation between George and the driver, consisting of what Peter thought were merely grunts, the driver set off to his next farm call.

Tea consisted of thick slices of home cooked ham and eggs that Marjorie fetched from the vast, cold pantry at the end of the kitchen. After tea, Marjorie explained that television reception was poor up on the moors and, as Peter was feeling decidedly weary after his busy day, he asked if it would be alright if he went to his room and read awhile before going to sleep. As it happened, he was asleep within ten minutes of getting into bed under a thick feather quilt.

In the morning, Peter woke up very early, before it was light, and decided to stay in his room rather than disturb Marjorie and George.

He dressed quickly in warm clothes and switched on the laptop. He was delighted to see that he was soon connected to a strong broadband signal. He sat at the big desk where, just out of interest, he looked up to see Friesian Cattle (he later learned that these cows were top quality and among the best milk producers). He read about the calves that George had talked about and decided that he wanted to see them again as soon as possible. He wanted to check on the one that was too weak to drink from the bottle.

He heard a scratching sound at his bedroom door and was immediately uncomfortable and somewhat scared. Peter went over to the door and opened it gingerly. Glen rushed in, greeted him enthusiastically and slipped under the desk, and appeared to fall asleep there. Peter sat at the desk again, being careful not to kick the sleeping sheepdog.

Peter did another search on his laptop for information about sheep. An article about uses for sheep's wool caught his eye and he was soon reading intently.

He found that he rather liked it when Glen woke up and nudged him until he stroked his lovely thick black and white coat. He was surprised that he didn't feel scared of the dog at all.

Peter heard welcome cooking noises from the kitchen below. Glen was awake and by the door in an instant and they both went downstairs into the very hot room where Peter was greeted by the biggest cooked breakfast he'd ever seen! He ate everything on his plate and drank two huge mugs of tea. He asked George about the milk yield from his dairy herd and was pleased that George agreed with everything that he had read online. He was a bit wary about asking questions about the calves, as he was sure that they were not long for this farm and would soon be in a cattle truck being driven miles to the cattle mart.

Peter made short work of his breakfast and his two mugs of very strong tea, before asking if he could go outside and look at the calves. George wasn't very good at hiding his pride in his livestock and, after kitting Peter out in a boiler suit and wellies, led him out to the calf shed, closely followed by Glen, Peter's new friend. George was very impressed when Peter studied each of the dozen or so calves very carefully and asked intelligent and pertinent questions about pedigrees, market prices and feed costs.

The weakest calf was back on its feet and Peter bottle-fed it with some warm milk. He discovered that he was loving close contact with the calf, despite it being a completely new experience that he would usually have found very unsettling for some considerable time.

"Your calves are very high quality and would be wasted if you sold them into the meat trade. From what I understand, it would be better to retain a small herd of the best animals and keep them as breeding stock, ready for selling on later in the year. The older cows could carry on as milk producers together with the some of the young female calves, once they've been put to the bull."

George was rather taken aback by the lads shrewd and accurate assessment of his Friesian herd.

"Have you been studying breeding and farm animals at school?"

"No, I did some research online this morning and made some notes about best practice on today's cattle farms. Have I said the wrong thing, George?"

"Not at all, Peter, you're spot on, I've been thinking along those lines myself, but I haven't had an opportunity to discuss it with anyone else."

"Can we go and look at the sheep now, please?"

"Of course. Hop in the Rangey."

George started up the battered old Range Rover, loaded Glen the sheepdog in the back and drove out of the yard, up a rutted track to the field where the sheep were grazing quietly. They mostly ignored Peter, George, Glen and the vehicle.

"What do you do with the fleeces?" Asked Peter abruptly.

"Well, we get in shearers from Cheshire and send the fleeces for processing as coarse low-quality wool for carpet making. We make no profit once we paid transport and the shearers, at least the ewes are comfortable in the hot weather."

Peter went quiet for a while and George convinced himself that he really wasn't interested in what happened to the wool at all. Perhaps he was just being polite. Abruptly, Peter started talking again.

"You'd be much better off joining the Staffordshire and Peak District Wool Co-op and selling the fleeces through them, into the house insulation trade. You'd get more money that way and you'd be helping the environment."

"Is that so, lad?" George was amused by the serious lad.

Peter didn't understand sarcasm and responded seriously.

"The transport comes from just down the road, takes all the fleeces into Sheffield where they are cleaned, and processed into thick insulation rolls. The driver collecting your wool pays you on the spot, in cash, and you don't have to haggle with the carpet firms on the phone for hours, the transport costs you nothing as well."

"Don't tell me lad, you looked all this up online before breakfast."

"That's right. Was that alright with you, George? I don't want to be rude."

"Nay, lad. What you say makes a lot of sense to me. It's time for a morning break now, I think you've earned it today."

"Excuse me, George, before we go back to the house, that ewe over there looks distressed. Is she OK?"

Leaving Glen tied up to a field gate, Peter and George walked cautiously across the field to the ewe lying awkwardly by the dry, stone wall. She tried to get up as they approached but slumped down to the ground with a muffled grunting sound.

George went up to her and gently felt each of her legs for any sign of injury.

"Well spotted my lad, she's got a damaged front left leg. Looks like she might have been chased by a dog and been bitten. If you hadn't noticed her, she might have died from an infected wound."

Peter crouched down by the stricken ewe and stroked her face. She relaxed immediately and let George spray some blue liquid on her damaged leg and allowed him to put a tight bandage on the wound. Peter was amazed when George bent down and swiftly heaved the stricken animal onto his back and set off back to the Range Rover. He put the ewe in the back with Glen, who seemed quite happy with the arrangement. They drove steadily down the farm track, trying not to cause further anxiety to the injured ewe.

When they arrived home, George shook off his wellies and set the ewe down in front of the Aga on an old rug. This didn't seem to be an unusual occurrence to Marjorie, and she was very pleased to hear that Peter had spotted the injured ewe from across the big meadow. The ewe seemed content to stay by the warm Aga and settled down and appeared to doze off. Glen crept under the table and nuzzled against Peter's leg. Marjorie and George noticed this new relationship but neither said anything.

* * *

Peter's stay on the farm seemed to him to feel like he was coming home. He continued to be very careful how he arranged his clothes in his room and still kept his lifelong habit of touching every door handle in the house as he passed by, but he relaxed contentedly into his new environment.

As the weeks passed, Peter spent a lot of his time both online and among the livestock, learning about their needs and how to care for them. He was thrilled when one morning George let him drive the old Ferguson tractor and trailer out to the hay field, with Glen sharing the driver's seat.

The weeks turned into months and George and Marjorie were in no rush to send him home to Salford. Peter never referred to his city family, nor seemed to want to make contact with them. They made no attempt to contact him either.

George became very aware that Peter had an intuitive way with the livestock and had long discussions with him and Marjorie in the evenings about issues with the individual animals. Peter spent much of his spare time online, reading up about various health issues that affected the Friesian cattle and the Gritstone sheep. He had conversations with George about the characteristics of various breeds.

Peter always got up early on a Thursday so he could get to the Farmer's Weekly, as soon as it landed on the doormat. He read each issue from cover to cover, sometimes he was in grave danger of missing his cooked breakfast! When George had finished reading Peter took them up to his room, where he stacked them in date order and made a note of the key articles in each copy on his laptop.

He was delighted when, on a routine visit, the local vet, Mick Fell, chatted to him as though talking to a veterinary colleague about a particularly difficult problem with one of the older ewes. Peter suggested a couple of issues with gritstone ewes that he had researched online, and Mick had to agree with him that he had diagnosed the issue that had stumped the local vets for some time.

As the New Year approached, the topic of formal schooling needed some discussion. After supper one evening, George asked Peter to sit in the hardly used lounge by a roaring log fire in the enormous black leaded grate. Nothing was said for a while, and then George broached the subject of a return to his boarding Special School for a term just until he was old enough to officially leave school.

No one could have predicted the effect this had on Peter. He flew into a hysterical rage, jumping to his feet, shouting and swearing at his uncle and aunt, scaring them witless. Neither of them had seen him in such a state. He threw himself about the room, accidentally smashing a couple of valuable vases. This scared the dog, who lay trembling by the solid wooden door, before Peter abruptly collapsed on the sofa trembling. George and Marjorie remained calm, despite being rather frightened by this outburst from their distressed nephew.

Almost as soon as it started, the terrifying rage was over and, for the first time since he arrived at the farm, Peter got off the sofa and threw himself into Marjorie's arms, sobbing hysterically.

Marjorie sat and held him for the rest of the evening. No one spoke and eventually, she led Peter up to his room, encouraging him to lie down, fully dressed, under his heavy quilt. He was asleep in seconds. George and Marjorie took it in turns throughout the night to sit beside Peter in case he woke up and needed someone to talk to.

At 5.30 in the morning, Peter and found himself alone. He got dressed and called out to his sleepy uncle that it was time to do the morning milking.

For the first time since he arrived on the farm, Peter worked in the parlour with George, skilfully milking the herd as though he had been doing this sort of work all his life. They worked in calm, companionable silence until it was time to head back to the house for breakfast. For a while, everyone ate in silence until there was a knock at the door that sent Glen off barking. It was Mick Fell, the vet, who wanted to talk to Peter.

Mick joined them at the table and accepted a cup of coffee offered by Marjorie. At last he turned to Peter.

"Peter, I've been thinking about this for some time now and I have a suggestion to make. I realise that you have not had a conventional education and your autism has been a problem for other people in your life."

Peter sat in stunned silence, wondering where this conversation was going.

"Your skill with the livestock is nothing short of amazing and your empathy with the individual animals is awesome. I realise that you have no formal qualifications at this time. We've discussed this back at the practice and my partners and I are willing, no, very keen, to offer you an apprenticeship with us, as soon as we can clear it with your family and the local veterinary authorities.

You will have to do all the dogsbody stuff, but we will include you in all the work that the partners do and, who knows, one day, if it's what you want, we think we could find a way to get you the basic qualifications to go to Veterinary College. We are prepared to negotiate a deal with Buxton College and furthermore, we will recruit, and pay for, a personal teaching assistant who has experience with autistic young people for you, as soon as you feel able to start College to work for your A Levels. You would be able to apply for Vet School in a year or so, if you still want to.

By the way, the pay will be terrible for a few years and the hours irregular and endless some days! I don't have to tell you that this is a mucky and dangerous job on occasions, but my partners will be furious with me if I don't go back to the office and say you agree to take up our offer after all the time I've spent talking about you with them since you arrived here."

Peter was ecstatic inside but reluctant to show or share his true feelings with his aunt, and uncle and Mick the vet. He sat staring at the floor for what seemed to his audience an age. Then, he looked around the room.

He spoke at last, in a very quiet voice, "I am so excited I'm not sure how to deal with it at the moment. This is the first time in my life anyone has believed in me and has not seen me as a problem that they can't be bothered to deal with."

"Is that a yes then, Peter?" Mick stood grinning like an idiot.

"Yes," said Peter.

Sue I'Anson

Sue I'Anson was born, raised and educated in Yorkshire.she worked first as a maths and IT teacher. Her husband's job meant that they were relocated several times (sometimes overseas), and so, taking whatever opportunity offered, she has worked as a pay clerk, a Kindergarten coordinator, a management information controller, an adult education tutor and an accounting technician. Happily retired and settled in Ripon, Sue enjoys writing short stories and poems, enviously reading other people's work, singing, solving cryptic crosswords and Sudoku puzzles, travelling and playing croquet, although not simultaneously.

It wouldn't be Christmas without…

Call me when it's over, tell me when it's done.
I hate this time of year, with its pressure to have fun.
It started several weeks ago but it's not Advent yet!
It shouldn't take so long to shop and get yourself in debt.
Christmas cards with Santas, candles, robins everywhere,
But stable scenes and wise men are becoming very rare.
As the day draws closer, the stress is catching hold;
Panic in the shopping aisles in case all stock's been sold.

The big day starts too early as the children are so keen
To open all those presents, assuming Santa's been.
Mum is in the kitchen as all the fun kicks off.
There's that turkey to attend to. Now which end do you stuff?
There are pigs to wrap in blankets, sprouts to trim, and spuds to peel.
(Thank goodness for the supermarket's BOGOF pudding deal).
By the time the meal is ready, her temper's really frayed
No one came to help her, but they'll eat the food she's made.

When the day at last is closing, all that will remain
Are cake crumbs, soggy sprouts and Grandad's indigestion pain.
The wrapping paper's torn to shreds, the crackers are all pulled,
There's turkey left to last the week, and only wine that's mulled.
By Boxing Day, the tinsel, lights and Christmas tree look sad,
Yet no one can remember when a better time was had.
I wonder why they do it – the celebrating thing.
Do they know the season marks the coming of a king?

This was inspired by too many conversations and increasing forgetfulness. We've all been there or are on the way…

Memory

Where have I put the thingamajig, I know that it was there
I put it on the whatsit, just before I combed my hair.
I might just make a shopping list, there is so much to get,
Visit the loo, put on my coat, and then I should be set.
I've so much to fit in each day and life moves on so fast.
No wonder I've forgotten things a few times in the past.
My brain is not declining, it's working just as well
As when we both were young, my dear. Now that just rings a bell…

Oh, I'd never have mislaid it if you weren't standing there
So impatient to be off and giving me a hostile stare.
I'll just go back to where I stood the last time that I had it.

Oh, here it is. I sometimes think that I am going mad.
It wasn't there last time I looked. I know it can't have been.
(It couldn't just be sitting there or else I would have seen.)
Before I shut the door, just check we've got the key,
Your library books, my handbag, the mobile… goodness me,
You quite forgot the thingy; we need that, no excuse.
I think that you'd forget your head, if only it were loose.

This piece is a remembrance of a typical day in the later 1950's, when I was a pupil at the local primary school.

A day in my life

I wake early. It is still dark outside, but I can hear the Co-op milk float as it makes its way along the road. There is a dull clunk as the tokens on our doorstep are replaced by bottles of icy cold milk. I pull the bedroom curtains aside and try to peer out, but I can see nothing but the feathery ice patterns on my side of the windowpane. I rub a small circle clear and am disappointed to see there is still no snow. Mum says it is too cold to snow. I expect she is right; she usually is!

I huddle back under the bedclothes and make plans for getting up. A clean vest and pants hang on the back of the chair. I dart out of bed, grab them and disappear quickly back to the warmth of my blankets. I'm prepared to wait a while until the icy chill is off them. With skill born of long practice, I wriggle out of my pyjamas and into my underwear, without breaking the surface of the sheets, and then brace myself for the rush to the bathroom. Once I have completed what are perforce very brief ablutions, I rush back to my room, scramble into my school uniform, and thence downstairs to seek the weak warmth of the fire in the living room. As always, Mum is there to brush my hair and tie my ribbon, before I address myself to a bowl of steaming porridge topped with my initials, marked out in evaporated milk. This, together with a cup of tea, ensures that my personal central heating is well and truly fired up.

I put on my gabardine mac, hat, scarf and gloves, readjust my long socks (which are always turning into short ones because my legs are skinny), and after warm kisses and hugs from Mum, I sally forth for the walk to school. Mum told me not to dawdle – it's too cold to do otherwise! Within ten minutes, I am sweltering in the heat of the school cloakroom, hastily peeling off my outdoor wear and trying to accommodate it all on one small peg. Around the cloakroom, and in most of the classrooms too, bottles of milk have been put on the central heating pipes to thaw them out. By break-time, the milk is usually over-thawed and distinctly cheesy!

The school day passes routinely, divided up by bells. The three R's are taught, tested, and reinforced, leavened with the occasional treat of being read a story, a lesson of country dancing, and compulsory time out in the fresh air. (The change of temperature plays havoc with my chilblains!)

Then at last it is time to go home. It is getting dark outside, and the streetlamps are being lit. The lamplighter is a dark figure – black raincoat, black trousers and boots, black bicycle. He cruises along the roads with a long pole balanced against his shoulder. He pauses at each lamp post like a dark hound and marks his territory by touching the gas mantle with the glowing fire at the pole's tip, to lighten the gloom.

Mum is waiting to hear all my news, help with my homework, whatever I need. She has made a comforting tea. The smell of toast makes my mouth water and I am silenced for a while as I eat my meal.

It seems to be bedtime all too soon. I get ready for bed and then come downstairs for a mug of Ovaltine, and the comforting "five minutes snugs" before I am dispatched to my room. I am asleep almost before I have created a warm nest under the bedclothes, and the cold of the night begins redecorating my windowpane.

Sunday – Past senses

The incense of crisping bacon and seared bread.
I stroll to Sunday school,
the church hall musty with memories.
Polished shoes clatter on bare boards;
the creaking of rickety chairs betrays our fidgeting.
Best behaviour almost exhausted,
we're released to return to earthly joys.

Rushing through our front door;
the aroma of roasting meat and potatoes,
the tang of chopped mint and the bass notes of gravy.
Not a moment too soon: the family feast,
our conversation interwoven with Forces Family Favourites.

Contented, a little drowsy, we clear the wreckage away.
Plates rattle dully in soapy water,
wiped dry, still warm, they sit in shiny ranks.
Duty done. Now off to the park!

Great palettes of bedding plants form coats of arms,
fragrant like hot pepper, basking in sunshine.
In the air, the babble of distant voices,
strained tinny music from the skating rink,
confident pomp from the bandstand.
All around, vast carpets of grass, bruised by my racing feet.

I can't take another step.
Sitting on a bench, the sun-scorched woodwork burns my legs.
O bliss! cooling creamy smoothness of ice-cream
with a waft of vanilla,
the creak-crack of sugar-wafers.
I am holding Dad's hand, so big, so strong,
I can make it home now.

This poem was prompted by a trip to Hunstanton and my insistence on going for a nostalgic paddle.

I must go down to the sea…….

Drawn down through dunes
sand cool, silky, yields to my feet
caresses,
then trickles dryly away.
Out onto the damp strand
scratchy, gritty, penetrates and lodges between my toes,
clings unwanted.

Stepping between discarded shells and flints
I reach the edge, crusted with finely ground shells and rock
all shape lost, crushed into uniformity.
Here the waves play Grandmother's Steps
approach hesitantly, then scuttle away
playfully fringe icy water with foam
gently, lovingly bathe my feet.

The slow heartbeat rhythm of waves soothes
until a stronger wave rises,
grasps my ankles, tugs me towards the vast featureless expanse of sea
menacing.
Held down by a sky turned grey
It's mesmeric, hypnotic.
I see the shallows soon plunge into deep water
and realise the deceit.
The enchanter means to gentle me,
lure me to a fatal underworld

yet I feel the call still …

Rulers of the deep

The boat set out in light and hope
and we with it,
excited, peering, pointing
but to no avail.

Our hunt slowed.
The light grew dim,
hope burned low.
We turned back sadly, subdued.

Then we saw them, gliding close
two, three, four massive shapes,
they rose, surfaced, dipped away,
performing a stately sarabande with gigantic grace
repeating their salute
to the silent drumbeat of the deep
awesome in their black and white majesty.

We made no sound.
Our two worlds drew close, kissed, parted.

Time ticked once more,
hearts resumed their rhythms,
but no soul was untouched, unmoved, unchanged.

I can't say what inspired this!

A stroke of luck

Where to begin?

He shouldn't have switched off the TV while I was watching Corrie. No, he shouldn't have been so rude about soaps, or housewives.

No, about me!

He shouldn't have spent all those years belittling me, bullying me, imprisoning me in the confined world of his idea of what a wife should be.

It served him right. It was his comeuppance. For once he was at **my** mercy. Out of luck there, George. Well, in one way he was lucky. I didn't lift a finger; never laid a hand on him.

They say he can hear me. The nurses at the hospital are so kind. They bring me tea and biscuits, which is more than he ever did! I sit by his bedside and let my thoughts wander. What does the future hold for him?

Who cares? He won't be coming home.

United?

What if the coach hadn't broken down? Well, maybe we would still be together.

It was a fiercely cold winter's day and that morning Bill and Eric had feared that the match might be called off. We were all relieved when Bill boarded the supporters' coach and headed off to United's away fixture in Sheffield.

I hurried back home and got ready. Showered, perfumed and dressed in the lingerie Eric had bought for me, I was trembling with anticipation. Promptly at noon, the doorbell rang and, having checked that it was in fact Eric, I opened the door and let him in. We didn't hesitate, not after planning this for so long, and were in each other's arms in seconds.

Well, I don't need to spell it out, do I? Love, or at least lust, ruled us and we were soon in bed together. It was about an hour later when I heard the front door open…

So, we're not together, Bill and I. It was a terrible time for us all, Eric included. He and Bill never spoke to each other again, and Eric begged his wife for forgiveness. They're still together, but he pays for being caught out, every day. As for me, I lost husband, lover and my sister. Bloody coach!

Judith Lonsdale

Judith Lonsdale is a writer and a poet. She started life with her feet firmly planted on the North East coast of England. She grew up looking out at silver skies and grey, marled sea mixed with the sound of seagulls, the clang of the shipyards and the clacking of tramcars. A little later in life she pulled up her roots, gathered her children and lived briefly in Cheshire before settling with her young family in the South. Always an avid reader, for many years writing had to be channelled into work and inspiration directed to letters and diaries, carefully kept for another day. Later life brought time to write. The carefully distilled thoughts were gradually freed. Living now in beautiful North Yorkshire, she has time to take pleasure in writing and poetry.

Street Portrait, 1950

Long, narrow street of joined-up houses,
drab shades of granite below grey slate,
silver in sunlight, pewter after rain.
Low, terraced cottages along one side,
tall, gaunt houses on the other.

No trees.

Bay windows concertina in a row,
ornaments and potted aspidistras on show.
Curtains draped with pattern facing out.
The front room framed proudly,
polished, preened but rarely used
except for priest, doctor, wedding or wake.

Sturdy front doors hide traditional lives.
Solid panels chamfered by a craftsman,
heavy brass doorknob too large for small hands,
polished letterbox for post and papers.
Behind is the porch door with china handle,
below jewelled panes of red, blue and amber.

Outside is a doorbell. The plate reads 'Press'.
Some have a bell pull, so tempting to try.
Run before the woman opens the door.
Don't stand on the step — chalky streaks not dry.
Just blame the cat who patted the gold-top,
leaving velvet paw prints
while the milkman's float purrs below clinking crates.

Men march abreast to the match on Saturday:
pavements worn by work-boots pounding,
heavy coats, mufflers tucked, caps over ears,
hot pie and Newcastle Brown at half-time.
Heads up as they go, downcast when they lose,
seeking solace in the pub, consolation later
from five Wild Woodbines and The Football Pink.

Weary women push prams, carry bags home.
Children mingle over marbles,
in gutters washed out by puddling pools;
play until twilight on cobblestones, calling
Charlie, can we cross the golden water
before rushing to safety on the other side
of a solid, Sunderland street.

Norfolk Watercolour

Leave me at the water's edge at dusk,
where withering grey sea hinges a skyscape,
lapping pools from worn-out dunes
then trickles back to restore morning's profile.

Soft fingers of slate and lavender hold up the sky,
catching phantoms of cloud before fading.

Oystercatchers scream eternal complaints.
Their banner of 'Kleep! Kleep!' streams above the horizon:
brushstrokes of beaks, legs and feathers,
eye-catching orange,
unexpectedly elegant pink,
alabaster white,
polished black,
swiftly setting the shades of marsh and sea
as hinterland.

Bereft

A wedding ring no longer worn
Rests on a velvet bed
Cold and small
Discarded

His token of tenderness
Lies uneasy
A circlet of questions
Lapsed

A wedding ring no longer worn
A roundel of rose gold
Empty
Finite

About Water

A sky of unpolished silver hangs low,
threatening biblical rain;
waits to souse the landscape.
Coursing water rises to meet ancient arches
of sturdy stone-built bridges;
thrashes every underside.
Surging water slakes the earth;
two elements become one.

Against an old stone wall,
hellebores stand to attention,
pale heads bowed.
Defiantly, they brave the deluge,
overseeing spikes of suppliant snowdrops.
Small titans.
Survivors.

Seventeen Seagulls: A Norse Skyline

A troubled sea slaps,
a fading light filters
greys through carbon black.

Inshore, dwarfed by snow-capped mountains,
a warehouse stretches gauntly to the quayside,
coiled ropes heaped ready to haul in cargo.

There, on the ridge of its red, metal roof,
seventeen seagulls, aquiline beaks to the sea,
knitted along the sky's edge,
patterned against pointed black.

They stand stock still,
a silent guard in this spiritual kingdom.

Surreal.

A Late Summer Lunch

Sheltering under the row of cypress trees, she glanced up at the house, wiping sweat from her neck. At the gateway, she heard a distant church bell chime three times: three o'clock. Her light shoes crunched across the drive, raising a powder of yellow dust. There were no cars to be seen. Wide stone steps led to a porch where heavy pots of geraniums soaked up the sun. A cat lay asleep in its shadow. As he stretched out in the languorous slow motion of deep sleep, a single flower detached itself and drifted down onto his ear. The cat twitched but the flower remained. She pulled the doorbell and listened as the noise clanged through the house. Inside, a telephone shrilled but was ignored. The cat slept on. The place was deserted.

She abandoned the front porch and followed a path around the side of the house. The telephone had stopped. Silence was restored. At the back of the house, there were tall windows overlooking the lawn. Closed. She walked on, registering the seductive scent of roses, warmed gently since dawn. The path narrowed and turned through a gateway of honeysuckle.

She found herself looking at all the signs of a late summer lunch. She caught her breath when she saw the table. With its rumpled tablecloth, empty wine bottles and abandoned plates it had the look of a leftover set from a provincial play…but it was the silk scarf that startled her. Draped over the back of a chair, it was unmistakably familiar, with its scarlet poppies against a pale grey background. Only one woman would wear it and she knew who it was. Her eyes took in the rest of the scene. Overhanging creepers cast shadows on the craggy stone wall and the worn, wooden door reflected the ochre light. There was a dead wasp floating in the bottom of the water jug.

The kitchen chairs had clearly been outside for days. Lunch was long over, and it was clear that no guest was expected.

Lucia first met Alfredo when she was a student at the music faculty. He was professor of singing and highly respected by his students and the professional world. Alfredo's protégés were welcomed worldwide. He immediately recognised her talent and steered her towards the competitive world of opera. It was thanks to him that she was now so successful. When she finally left, he made her promise to return.

The invitation had been clear. The next time she was in Tuscany, she was to present herself for lunch on the very first Sunday afternoon. She recalled his words and his smile, 'I keep summer Sundays for my friends – lunch in the garden and the sun. I will expect you.' She kept her promise. She was here in a deserted garden. Where was he?

With her mind full of self-reproach, she sat on one of the chairs. Leaving a telephone message on a Friday was always a risk. Alfredo had probably not even attended the department that day. If only she had sent a card last week confirming her intention to visit, all of this could have been avoided.

Thinking, she stretched out her arm along the back of the chair. Her fingers touched the silk scarf which wavered in the sun, releasing a light scent.

Before she could stop herself, she recalled the scene she had worked so hard to forget.   It was tradition for each department to offer entertainment after dinner at the end of the summer term. It was always a mixture of musical delights which reflected the talents of each student. As the evening wore on and the wine flowed, everyone relaxed and people shared their future hopes. Alfredo was a legendary host who captured the hearts of many a young singer before the professional world lured them away. That evening she had sung with her friends, to the delight of Alfredo. As time went by, Alfredo asked her to sing alone. Nervously, she prepared to do so. As the opening bars of the introduction filled the air, she saw that

Alfredo's face had frozen. Her music faded out as, from the shadows, came the mournful sound of a traditional fado song. Rosa stepped into the softly lit space at the centre of the group. She was wearing a black crepe dress which moulded to her shape. It had the suggestion of a ruffle at the hem. Around her shoulders she wore a grey silk wrap, over-printed with a swathe of scarlet poppies. She walked as she sang, filling the space with her sad and poignant song. Everyone was transfixed as she gazed at Alfredo, directing the heart-rending fado at his very soul. When the song ended there was a moment of perfect silence, while a single tear trickled down the face of Alfredo.

Lucia's moment was gone.

Rosa kissed her hands at her unwitting audience. Alfredo rose to welcome her, making space beside himself for her to join him.

To bring the painful memory to a close, Lucia stood up and ran her fingers through her hair. It was time to go. She should never have come here in the first place. Why had she ever thought that Alfredo wanted to see her? Why had she continued to believe in him after that evening when he had seemed so reluctant to explain the sudden arrival of Rosa? She needed to walk away from the shadow of Rosa, once and for all. Slowly, she turned her back on the deserted loggia and retraced her steps through the honeysuckle archway to the front terrace. The cat was still sleeping as she passed by the door. Lucia walked along the dusty road to where she had left the car. The warmth inside was overpowering, even though the windows were down. She stretched over the driver's seat to pick up a bottle of water and drank the warm contents with relief. Somewhat comforted, she reached into her handbag for the keys. As her hand touched on the keys, she knew what she had to do. She quickly wrenched the fob away from the ring. It was one of a series of sentimental name plates and hers read, 'Lucia Lirica'. Alfredo had once picked up her keys from the floor and returned them to her with a wry smile and a comment about a fitting label for an opera singer. Lucia got out of the car and made her way back to the house. As she walked, she attached the key fob to a card printed with the details of her hotel. She left this makeshift calling card on a small china dish on the table and hoped that Alfredo would find it.

Time went by. Discreet enquiries about Alfredo came to nothing. It was as though he had disappeared. Lucia was puzzled but resigned herself to accepting that the story was over.

The following summer brought a surprise invitation to Lucia. She was invited to audition for La Traviata, which was being staged at the beautiful little opera house in Bologna. As such opportunities usually require a recommendation, she wondered how her name had been selected. When she was successful, she was ecstatic and packed her bags for the performances in Bologna.

She was booked into a hotel close to the theatre and arrived there in plenty of time to find her way about the city. The Angelus bells started to ring just as she reached her room. She drew back the curtains and threw open the long windows. The golden warmth of Italy spread inside, lighting up shades of rose and ochre. She breathed in deeply, then stepped forward and looked out over the busy piazza. Students were walking purposefully on their way to and from lectures, some eating pizza or gelato.

Three young people arrived in the piazza and parked their bicycles. The girls carefully connected with the bike stand, locking their wheels. The boy attended to cooling down his body, lifting the cream and green striped vest and letting the air to his oiled flesh. His black shorts were rolled up and his cycle undershorts looked like black tubes. With a billow of their cool cotton sundresses, the girls went off to find a coffee shop, leaving the boy to secure his bike. He was in no hurry, lingering to adjust his sunglasses. A dapper, older man wearing a brown suit was carrying a leather bag with a strap, a half portfolio, half briefcase. Perhaps he was a professor, wending his way to the music faculty, just out of sight. From further up the Via Zamboni came the gliding tones of a lone accordion player. The melody was waltz-like, softening the air and blending beautifully with the blushing shades of gold and terracotta on the ancient porticoed streets. Lucia sighed, beautiful Bologna, offering such promise.

Over the two weeks, there were seven performances of La Traviata and Lucia was greeted successively with rapturous applause. In all too short a time, she found herself anticipating the last night. That morning, as she went to breakfast, she was given an envelope. Seated later with her coffee, she slipped her fingers under the embossed flap and drew out a printed card. The address was the very house she had visited on that Sunday afternoon last summer. The flowing writing was a hand she recognised all too well and the words were an invitation to supper after the last performance. It was signed 'Alfredo'.

There were many curtain calls that evening and Lucia knew that she would never forget such a memorable experience. As usual, there were loud calls of appreciation from the audience and many flowers. As the bouquets were presented, a single rose was slipped into her hand. Attached to the ribbon around its stem was a card on which was written, 'I await you, please do not disappoint.'

The Walled Garden

It was a lacklustre morning. The sky was grey and there was no sun. A hint of sea fret blowing in from the coast made him pull his woollen hat down over his ears. This was the time of day he liked most. At first light, everything was his to savour while others slept.

The early mornings were even more precious when the nights were drawing in. This morning, he remembered the old days working at the Hall. No sooner had he pedalled to work through the camouflage greens and browns of a winter's morning, than he seemed to be on the return journey with an eye to the amber lights of home.

Cuthbert couldn't remember a day when he had doubted his chosen job. As a small boy, he had always known that he was going to carry on the work of his father and grandfather before him and work in the gardens of Lambsdale Hall. The old house had stood proudly for hundreds of years. Its grounds stretched out over acres of fine land renowned for its natural beauty.

In the past, there had been at least a dozen gardeners to tame and tend the earth. His grandfather had been the master gardener as the century had turned. Later, his own father had spent the whole of his working life in the hot houses. Those were the days when cut flowers were needed in profusion for the many social occasions of the year and exotic fruits, imported as tender plants from the Colonies, were expected to inspire the cook and grace the table.

Now times were different. Country houses had to earn their keep and Lambsdale Hall was no exception.

The latest development had arrived with the millennium. The old walled kitchen garden, long fallen into disuse, was to be revived as a working model for the nearby Royal Horticultural College. Their students had been given the brief of designing and developing the entire project. It was going to be a long job as the planting and cultivation were to be spread over the natural seasons of the year.

A television documentary team had been assigned to follow the process of bringing the garden back to life. Eventually a series of programmes would hit the screens of the nation and there would be the usual glossy book out just in time for Christmas.

There had been steady interest in the local newspaper and even on national radio. The run up to next Christmas would bring a large amount of publicity to the estate and, the Trustees hoped, a great deal of money.

That was one of the reasons why Cuthbert's morning was overcast. Some weeks ago he had received a letter from the TV company asking him to lend his support towards the documentary. Cuthbert had mixed feelings about the whole business. It was mostly to do with respect. When he had retired from the gardens almost twenty years ago, he had resolved to let Lambsdale go. The arrival of the letter had somehow proved more difficult than he expected. As the sole surviving gardener from a family long connected with the grand old days of Lambsdale he could remember when the land was worked by men whose knowledge of nature was instinctive. They were men rightly in awe of the seasons and for whom Harvest Home was a true celebration. How could he possibly reconcile the principles of a lifetime and allow himself to be drawn into being part of a television documentary called 'Evergreen'?

The traditionalist in him would never let him understand how a few students could possibly begin to restore the walled garden. It was a special place to him and he wasn't sure that he wanted any do-gooding TV company meddling in his memories for the sake of entertainment. Working the land required dedication and respect for ritual. In his imagination he winced as he saw strangers trampling recklessly over the earth he had tended so traditionally and respectfully in his time. Someone had told him that nowadays girls were allowed into these fancy modern horticultural colleges and he found himself wondering what was wrong with a good old-fashioned apprenticeship as a gardener's lad or a gardener's lass.

In the end, his curiosity had got the better of him. If there was to be a revival, then he had to be part of it and today was the day when he was to meet the producer. That was another irritation. How could some slip of a London woman possibly understand the spirit of 'his' garden. Only he knew its secrets. Then there were the students to meet. Grudgingly, he assented that they sounded more promising because at least they had chosen a career in the soil. He would enjoy telling them how it used to be in the olden days of practical horticulture. He was determined to enjoy putting paid to their modern theories.

It had been a long time since he had made this journey, but the old bike and the older body were doing well. As he drew closer to the gates, he was pleased to see that nothing had changed. Everything seemed to be in order. He pedalled along the perimeter wall to the stone gateway and let himself into the gardeners' entry that led past the old coach house to the bothy near the potting sheds. It was here that a soft voice from the doorway greeted him through the silence.

"Hello, hope I didn't startle you. I'm Cathy, from Northern TV. I thought I'd come and meet you here so that we could make a good start. We've met but I don't know whether you remember me?"

Cuthbert looked up from his bike into the face of a smiling woman. She was wrapped up well against the chill morning air and had what his father would have called 'roses' in her cheeks. He had not forgotten. He was conscious of the rubber soles of her Wellington boots thudding over the stone pathway. In her hands were two mugs of steaming tea. She held out one to him.

"I thought you might be ready for this."

He took it gratefully.

This was not what he had expected. He heard his disembodied voice thanking her for her kindness and telling her, of course he remembered her growing up at the house, but his head was simply not registering that this was real.

How could he ever forget Catherine? Hadn't he always loved her, ever since he had watched her grow up at Lambsdale? He remembered sunny afternoons in the garden when she came as a child to help him. In the end, he had made a little garden just for her. It was in the southwest corner where the sun was always warm. He recalled the day when they had found the old stone words hidden under the moss on the wall. He had read them to her. After that, she would never go back into the house for tea until she had read the words to him.

He looked up at her with a slow smile on his face as she said, "Come and meet the students. They're really looking forward to hearing about how it used to be. Oh, we found something yesterday that I think you'll remember. I certainly did. It was in the sunny corner of the garden. Part of the wall had crumbled there so we had the stonewallers in to see what we could salvage. Underneath all the buried debris they found the big stone with the words carved on it. I'll show you later if you'd like to see it."

Cuthbert barely had time to swallow before they were through the gateway and inside the walled garden. He found himself looking at a group of warm and smiling faces.

The whole group of young men and women were on their feet and clapping as they came across the grass to meet him.

In that unforgettable greeting all his apprehensions disappeared. The voice of his grandfather came back to him, proudly recalling what his fine gardeners used to manage. Cuthbert looked at his team and felt himself grow younger and taller as he moved towards them.

Suddenly he recalled the old stone words:

Hours fly
Flowers die
New days
New ways
Pass by
Love stays

Now it was his turn to be proud to have moved with the times. At last, he was back in the walled garden: content and honoured to be there.

The *old stone words* are attributed to poet Henry Van Dyke.

Marla Skidmore

Marla Skidmore grew up in a small medieval city in the Yorkshire Dales. After living in Europe for a number of years, she returned home to become a mature student and on completion of her studies, became a College Lecturer. A History enthusiast, she is fascinated by the people and events of the past and this is reflected in much of her writing. Her award-winning debut novel, 'Renaissance – The Fall and Rise of a King,' – inspired by the discovery of Richard III's remains in 2012, gives the reader an entirely new perspective on this controversial king. She is now involved in two projects – researching and writing a sequel to 'Renaissance,' the story of Francis Viscount Lovell – King Richard's closest friend and a romantic, murder mystery set during the Peninsula Wars. When not immersed in her novels, Marla also enjoys writing short stories and poems, tending her large garden, exploring ancient ruins and taking long walks with her West Highland Terrier in the countryside surrounding the Dales village where she now lives.

The Stripper

In the wake of summer's exuberant frolic
hers is a gradual entrance upon Nature's stage.
Veiled behind swirling mists and hazy skies
she glides seductively over the landscape,
entrancing us with sensuous beauty.

The crimson and gold of her costume
steals away our breath and beguiles our eyes,
blinding us to the reality beneath the glamour.

Slowly, sinuously Autumn sheds her garments
glorious colours drift softly to the ground.
When her disrobing is complete
the gnarled and withered limbs of a dying year are revealed.

Elegy

Gone!
You've not passed into a better world,
You won't be waiting on the other side,
Only ashes.
Only dust.

And yet, while my tears flow, become a lake of grief
I trace the contours of your face, high among the landscapes of sunlit
clouds.

Your essence surrounds me as I watch summer shadows play in the
twilight garden
Night wind becomes the soft sigh of your breath against my cheek.

In the silence before dawn, you dance along corridors of my mind,
I hear the echo of your laughter, your voice whispering 'forget me
not.'

You are gone.
Your body lies beneath the ground
But as long as I draw breath,
You are not dead.
You live…in me.

Battlefield Tour

Culloden; packaged and presented.
A shiny hi-tech visitor centre,
where neat stone footpaths guide the curious
over a tamed Drummossie moor,
for "The Perfect Battlefield Experience".

But when the sun dips behind the mountains
and each clan stone sinks into its own deep shadow.
Stop.
Listen.
You will feel a nation's agony.
Weep, as once more through an icy April mist,
you see Bonnie Charlie's Highlanders
struggle through clutching bog and biting bracken
to meet Cumberland's belching cannon
and death at the point of a bayonet.
The command, "Give no quarter!" echoing down the years.

In under an hour it was done.
What remains?
A sense of honour abandoned?
The desolate ache of betrayal?
The legacy of a dreamer who seduced the people
and left them in a wasteland of tears.

Ruined

They renewed their vows,
walked away from sinful society;
made their home in the wild lonely valley of the Skell.

In this cruel world, thick with thorns
and ragged rocks,
Nature, not humanity, held sway.
Here the babble of men was absent;
they could hear the Creator's voice
in the tumbling river,
the chattering of the jackdaw; the howling of the wolf.

Heaven smiled on the White Monks;
they made the wilderness bloom
and the desert bring forth plenty.
Wealth and power was their reward,
seducing them from their simple piety.
Then the jealous gaze of a king turned their way.

Now, from roofless walls,
empty arched windows
stare bleakly over manicured lawns,
watching as throngs of summer visitors
clamber incuriously over sacred stones.

The lamentation of a tolling bell echoes across the valley.

Waiting for Papa

Isaac strode eagerly down the gangplank gazing up and down the quayside. Two years had gone by since the ship had last put into this little fishing port that he called home. Nothing had changed in his absence. Trawlers still waited to go hunting herring at the turn of the tide and weathered old fishermen still sat on the jetty in the sunshine, earning their ale by mending nets and sails.

He had five days of shore leave in which to make his peace with Emmy. Settling his heavy kitbag into a more comfortable position on his broad shoulders, Isaac moved purposefully along the cobbled streets that spread, like the tentacles of an octopus, behind the harbour. She would be in their stone cottage with the bright green door and the whitewashed step. The man who was returning to her was very different from the miserable creature that had left her to fend for herself. The Navy had straightened him out; given him back his self-respect. He was ready to face her now; to care for her as he should have done in the past. The prize money he had tucked away in the bottom of his kitbag would buy her all the comforts and pretty things she deserved but had for so long gone without.

As Isaac walked along the familiar winding streets, bitter and painful memories raced through his mind of that terrible summer when he'd lost his job. It had been a blow, but he'd not worried much, at first. He had been sure he'd swiftly find another trawler berth. How misplaced his confidence had been. Summer turned to Autumn and Autumn to Winter and still his search for work continued to be fruitless. He'd tried every fishing port along this coastline, but every captain gave him the same regretful refusal. Fish prices had slumped; they weren't taking on crew. Becoming more and more desperate, he'd trudged inland, hoping to find work on a farm, to no avail. Harvests were bad. Farmers were letting their own workers go, much less taking on any new labourers. The odd day's casual work here and there barely kept the wolf from the door and as time passed, many of their possessions had ended up in the pawnshop. As they struggled to get by, his wife and pretty daughter became paler and thinner with each passing day. Their cosy home became a cheerless place and his sweet vivacious wife turned into a hard-faced demanding shrew, who mocked him at the end of each soul-weary day for his inability to provide for them. The one bright star in that miserable existence was his young daughter, Emmy. She always welcomed him home with a smile and a kiss.

One evening, at the end of another long exhausting day unsuccessfully trying to find work, he had returned home to find his wife gone. After shutting Emmy into the big cupboard beneath the stairs with her ball and favourite rag doll, she'd taken everything that she could still sell and left. He'd turned to drink then. Alcohol gave him a brief escape from poverty and fear. Whenever he'd managed to earn a few coppers, he'd spend most of them in the smoky cheerful alehouse, drinking himself into oblivion. Emmy strove to keep their home together. She cleaned their cottage and prepared their meagre meals. She never uttered a word of complaint when he drank away what little money, he did manage to earn but sometimes, when he returned home from a day's casual labour, reeking of ale and with empty pockets, she couldn't hide her tears.

How he'd hated those feelings of shame and guilt that battered him whenever he opened the front door and looked into her hungry face, knowing he'd let her down again. One cold and dreary evening, his feelings of frustration, humiliation and guilt became too much. Pent-up emotions boiled over and he released his fury upon his vulnerable child. Afterwards, he'd reeled out of the cottage as fast as his unsteady legs could carry him. All he'd wanted to do was to return to the noisy companionship of the alehouse and forget everything. Later that night, as he had drunkenly staggered back home, he'd stumbled straight into the arms of the Press Gang.

Isaac let himself into the cottage.

"Emmy?"

Disappointed at not finding her at home, he looked around. The house felt empty and neglected, which was strange because Emmy always liked to keep the cottage as neat as a new pin, but he wasn't too worried. Press gangs operated regularly in this port. The neighbours would have taken her in and looked after her as soon as they realized the Navy had pressed him into service. Dropping his kitbag to the floor, he lowered himself into the familiar shabby armchair that stood beside the empty range. He was tired – he'd just rest for a bit and then go and find her. As he drifted off to sleep, he wondered what the strange pit-pat, pit-pat, pit-pat sound echoing through the house was.

Gentle hands shook Isaac awake. Slowly, he opened his eyes to the familiar wrinkled face of his neighbour Annie Harris.

"Annie, where's my Emmy? You know that you have my grateful thanks and shall have a share of my prize money for taking care of her whilst I was away."

Annie's faded blue eyes filled with tears. She wrung her hands and swallowed hard. There was no way to spare him the truth.

"She's dead Isaac," she choked out tearfully. "At first, when you both disappeared, we thought you'd left town taking Emmy with you. We didn't think to check the house. A few weeks had gone by, when one of the trawler men spotted you out in the Channel on the riggings of HMS Relentless, but then it was already too late."

Isaac stared uncomprehendingly at her for a long moment; he blinked as the horror of what she was telling him seeped into his brain. Emmy was dead! He choked back the cry of anguish rising in his throat. His mind screamed How could this be? After her mother's desertion, he had drummed into Emmy that she was to seek out Annie, if ever he failed to return home. Grief ripped through him. Isaac buried his face in his hands; rocking back and forth, he wept bitterly. Her face bleak with sorrow, Annie's gnarled, work-worn hand pressed down upon his shoulder.

"We gave her a decent burial Isaac and I've been putting fresh flowers on her grave every week. Come. I'll take you to her now."

Later that night, as a broken-hearted Isaac roamed restlessly around the dark and desolate cottage, he heard again the mysterious sound he'd fallen asleep to earlier.

Pit-pat, pit-pat, pit-pat.

It continued relentlessly; the steady rhythmic beat began to pound inside his head until he felt it would explode. He searched each shadowed room, only to find nothing. Icy fingers of fear skittered up and down his spine. Holding his candle aloft Isaac slowly made his way back down the wooden stairs towards the front parlour. When he neared the bottom, he noticed that the sound seemed to be coming from beneath his feet. Terrified, he halted and listened, afraid to even breathe. He plucked up enough courage to wrench open the door of the under stairs' cupboard. Nothing. The sound continued to beat out its incessant rhythm. As he stood there, staring blankly into the void, a tearful childish voice began to whisper repeatedly in his ear.

"I'm waiting for papa. He'll be coming home very soon."

The voice of his dead daughter echoed around the house. Isaac fell to his knees and prayed for forgiveness, as the memory of what he'd done to Emmy on that fateful night came flooding back vividly. In his drunken rage, he'd thrust and locked Emmy into the cupboard. As a sop to his conscience, he'd thrown her rag doll and ball in with her, and then he'd staggered back to his drinking friends in the alehouse. While she had waited for her papa to come home and release her from her imprisonment, his lonely little daughter had passed the time away by bouncing her ball off the cupboard wall. He hadn't returned and she was bouncing it still.

A Hint of History

Greenwich Palace Spring 1510

"Play-on!"

The imperious command was given by a golden-haired giant to the musicians in the gallery above his head.

"Play a Pavane in honour of our queen."

Henry Tudor swung on his heel and strode down the length of the Great Hall leaving the young woman, whom he had been partnering in a country-dance, to stand alone in the middle of the massive chamber. He halted abruptly in front of an arched doorway, through which the dainty figure of Queen Catherine had just made her entrance, followed by her ladies-in-waiting. She placed a slender, white hand into his outstretched palm and curtsied deeply. Raising eyes of a startling blue to look into her husband's handsome face, Catherine smiled radiantly at him.

"Sire, I am honoured that you would dance the stately dance of the country of my birth, when I know you favour the faster steps and twirls of the Italian dances."

Henry's narrow lips pursed and his small hooded eyes, of a much paler blue than those of his wife, ran speculatively over her small frame.

"Aye, but we have a care for your health madam. You have only lately returned to us after a fruitless confinement and long weeks of sickness."

The Court collectively winced at the carelessly spoken, hurtful words. Everyone at court, down to the most insignificant kitchen scullion, knew of their beloved young queen's heartache at having miscarried her first child and of her long struggle back to good health.

"You took to your bed, having lost my heir," Henry's broad features took on a sullen expression. "My Court was left without a queen. It was most inconvenient," he complained peevishly. "We would not wish you to overtax yourself and endanger your health by undertaking any energetic activities too soon, for you could succumb to the malady once again!" In front of the whole Court, Henry made Catherine's recent miscarriage and subsequent poor health appear an act of self-indulgence – a failure of her queenly duty.

Catherine paled at the egotism behind his words. They fuelled her acute sense of loss that was a physical pain, whenever she thought of her lost baby son. For a long silent moment, she studied her husband's petulant face. Blinking away hot tears, she straightened her spine, lifted her small, determined chin and raised herself to her full diminutive height. In a soft, haughty voice, that left no doubt in anyone's mind that they were in the presence of a princess of Spain, the daughter of Ferdinand and Isabella, Catherine responded to her husband's self-centred lack of compassion.

"It was the will of God that the babe came too early and did not live; nor was I sick from choice your Grace." The formal dignity of her words, and the icy tone in which they were spoken, made everyone hold their breath.

How would their spoiled, young king take this reprimand? Was the Court to witness the first royal quarrel of a marriage, many felt Henry had made too hastily, after his accession to the throne, and others, more romantically inclined, maintained was made in heaven?

Instead of the expected explosion of temper, which was Henry's usual reaction to being opposed, he dropped his head and fiddled with the bejewelled handle of the dagger hanging at his side. Shuffling his feet, he finally looked sheepishly into his wife's coolly composed face. Everyone then remembered that he was after all, still only eighteen years old, six years Catherine's junior.

Enfolding her tiny hand between his large paws, he pulled her closer and bent his lofty frame to whisper, "I missed you!" Your sickness frightened me!" They wouldn't allow me to see you! I was all alone and had to manage everything without you. I needed you beside me!"

She heard the self-pitying insecurity in his voice and recalled that, unlike herself, who had known from infancy that she would one day become queen of England, and had been prepared for this role from the cradle, Henry, until the death of his brother, had been only a second son, neglected and ignored by his father. He had received no training in kingship, and until Arthur's death, had grown up in his mother's Court, indulged and petted by his mother and grandmother. Her heart softened. After all, he was little more than a boy. He had been her staunch friend and ally during her long poverty-stricken widowhood and on his accession to the throne, had insisted on their immediate marriage in the face of much opposition from his dead father's Councillors. Their eyes met; Catherine realized that this was as close as she would get to receiving an apology from him.

"I am fully recovered and will remain so," she assured him in a calm voice.

"Are you really well again?" Henry asked earnestly, studying her face for telltale signs of illness. Her reply was emphatic.

"Yes, your Grace! I shall join you for the Hunt on the morrow. If you permit?"

Henry looked doubtful. "You are well enough to ride?"

"Be at ease Sire," Catherine firmly pushed aside his hesitation. "I am returned to my old-self once more!"

A feeling of immense relief washed through him. His world had righted itself again. The person upon whom he totally relied was back by his side where she belonged. Henry beamed in delight. He bowed low over Catherine's hand, kissed her slight fingers and then her smooth cheek. She squeezed his hand in reassurance.

The king signalled once more to the gallery. The musicians struck up. He turned to lead the queen into the dance, but she held back laughing.

"Not the Pavane, Sire! We are young…it is May-time!" she exclaimed. "Let us celebrate our youth, spring and my return to Court with a joyful dance."

"The Volta then!" Henry shouted enthusiastically.

He bowed once more to his queen and the courtiers made room for their energetic young king to display his dancing prowess. Encouraged by Catherine, Henry danced, his fast footwork and high leaps making her laugh and clap her hands, then gasp in mock fear when he grasped her around the waist and lifted her high into the air. The whole Court joined their king and queen in the dancing, the Great Hall of the old palace became a vivid moving tapestry as the richly embroidered doublet and hose of the gentlemen merged with the jewel-like colours of the ladies' swirling skirts.

Thomas More, newly appointed Under Sheriff of London, propped his shoulders against a convenient doorframe and waited for an opportune moment to pay his respects to his royal master. From this vantage point, he had watched in admiration for the way in which the young queen had dealt with her volatile husband. Noting the sullen pout of the king's small mouth turn into a wide smile of delight, as he led her into the dancing. Thomas was content with his decision to support Henry's hasty marriage to the widow of his elder brother. It was a wise one. Catherine's maturity and diplomacy would restrain his temper, his extravagance and his lust for glory.

Thomas's thoughts turned to the old king's advisers, now languishing in the Tower. They could have taken lessons from this woman, whom they had dismissed as a nuisance for so long. To their own cost, these men had entirely misread their new master's character. They thought that his youth and inexperience would allow them to manipulate him and continue with the parsimonious policies of their defunct regime. Henry may have been young and untried, but he was an egoist with a formidable intellect, who was determined to make his mark on the world. There was no doubt in Thomas's mind that Henry, now in possession of the over-flowing coffers of the royal treasury, would turn his father's tired Court into a glittering showcase that would dazzle the rest of Europe. The reign of the most handsome prince in Christendom and his pretty Consort would ensure peace, stability and prosperity for England. He was young and virile. She had proven herself fertile and although the child had died, there was time-a-plenty for young Harry to sire more little princes upon her. The future was bright indeed.

...but what did the future hold for Henry VIII, Catherine of Aragon and Sir Thomas More? In the far distance, thunder clouds were gathering for all the Players in this drama.

Military Manoeuvres

Waterloo Barracks, Catterick Garrison – August 1999

The drowsy silence of a hot Sunday afternoon was shattered by the chatter and laughter of a lively group of teenagers emerging from the tall austere buildings surrounding the parade square. They all had the slightly damp and rumpled appearance of recent swimmers. Henry Tennant, who had joined his parents in their new posting for the school holidays, pushed Armani sunglasses back over his carefully styled hair and turned towards the imposing building of the Officers' Mess.

"That was fun…can't remember when I last played water polo. It's made me really thirsty though. I could murder an ice-cold Coke," he announced, moving forward to the empty square.

"Whoa there! Don't go across the square! The RSM will have your guts for garters!" A tall loose-limbed youth grabbed Henry's arm. Daniel Garret's dark young face was lit by an infectious grin. "It's obvious that you've not been here very long, or you wouldn't even consider crossing 'God's Acre,' he chuckled.

"God's Acre…? What on earth are you babbling about?" demanded Henry shaking off Daniel's arm impatiently. He was hot and thirsty and wanted that Coke now. The quickest way to get it was to cut across the parade square.

Dan's eyes twinkled wickedly. "Your military education seems to be sadly lacking. You should know by now that the Regimental Sergeant Major is God and that the parade square is his fiefdom. No-one, but no-one, walks across it without his permission…" he paused dramatically… "Ever!" The others couldn't resist some friendly teasing.

"You'll be marched, double time in front of the RSM, made to stand
to attention and explain your heinous crime," giggled Dan's twin
sister Sophie, as small and dainty as her brother was tall and gangly.

"Then he'll make you scrub the square with a toothbrush," added
James Cartwright, the padre's son mischievously, his bespectacled
face creasing into an impish grin at the thought of elegant, fastidious
Henry, down on his knees on the vast dusty square, scrubbing away
with a tiny toothbrush.

Henry was not amused. He hated being at a disadvantage, the butt of
a joke or the source of amusement for others. He turned a furious
face towards the laughing group of friends. "Don't be so bloody
juvenile! he snapped. "I'm the Commanding Officer's son! What can
he actually do if I choose to ignore his stupid rule and just walk
across his precious square… he's not even an officer! He can't order
me about…and had better not try!" he sneered.

The light-hearted banter stopped abruptly and in the ensuing silence,
all eyes turned towards the thin, red-haired girl, who had just
rounded the corner to join the group. "Oh lord! Bobby is bound to
have heard that tirade against her dad," muttered Sophie.

Daniel grimaced. "Wow! You have a really great way of making
friends," he observed in a dry undertone."

The uneasy silence lengthened. The rest of the group eyed each other
nervously – how was she going to react? Their Bobby was a bit of a
tomboy and had a temper that matched her fiery hair. She and her
dad were really close, her mum having died when she was a baby. It
wouldn't matter to her that Henry was the Commanding Officer's
son. If she felt he was attacking her dad, she would go after him with
all guns blazing!

For a long moment Roberta Harrison's sherry-coloured eyes studied
Henry, then she shrugged her shoulders. "My dad's only upholding
regimental traditions," she reflected calmly. "I think you'll find that
your father won't thank you if you flout them and put him in a

difficult position." They all breathed a sigh of relief. Bobby was not going to punch his nose or rip him to shreds with her wicked tongue – this time.

Dan gave Henry a little push from behind. "Now would be a good time to grovel a bit," he murmured. Henry shot him a look of acute dislike and said nothing. "Look…you've dug yourself into a hole. Now dig yourself out, sharpish!" Dan ordered, exasperated. "We are all going to be spending the summer together. Bad feelings between you two will make all of us uncomfortable." Henry remained silent. He was seething inside, Dan the son of a major, was siding with a ranker's brat against him!

"Let him be Dan. I don't need an insincere apology from him and whether he crosses the square or not is entirely up to him." Bobby turned away and began to follow the others who were swiftly putting distance between themselves and the tense situation, by rapidly making their way around the square to the Officers' Mess.

"You are a prat, Henry!" You've disrespected Mr Harrison, who's a great guy. If I were you, I'd start thinking about how to put matters right." Dan shook his head and hurried to catch up with Bobby.

"I'm parched! I need my coke-fix quick!" Sophie leapt up the wide steps to the entrance of the Mess, the others enthusiastically following suit.

"Wait!" Henry's imperious tone stopped everyone in their tracks. They turned around to find him looking disdainfully at Roberta. "You can't come in here," he said smugly. Bobby looked back at him in bewilderment. "Your father might be the god-like RSM, but his power ends here. He's still a man from the ranks and only allowed into the Mess on duty or by invitation from the Commanding Officer." Henry grinned at her maliciously. "Therefore, as his brat, the Mess is out of bounds to you too."

"You have to be joking!" Dan glared angrily at Henry, unable to believe his sheer spite. "Bobby's always been welcome in this Mess.

Colonel Ellis's wife coached her in the library for the Oxbridge exam; when Bobby was awarded her Oxford bursary, she held a party for her here."

"That was then; this is now. There's a new regime in place." Henry smirked. "I'm only following military rules. You know as well as I do, Daniel, that other ranks are not allowed into any Officers' Mess – except to work, of course."

He couldn't resist twisting the knife. "The only way you will be able to come in here from now on, is if you were to apply for a job here…as a waitress or a cleaner. Quite a few wives and daughters of enlisted men work here in the Mess." He laughed into Bobby's stricken face and pushed past her into the Mess. He called back over his shoulder. "Don't presume to be as good as your betters Roberta Harrison. Stay amongst your own kind."

The opportunity to humiliate the RSM's stuck-up bitch of a daughter had given him enormous satisfaction. *She might be a bloody genius going to Oxford, but she was still from the ranks. How dare she presume to teach him, who came from a family whose sons had been commissioned into this regiment for generations, about regimental traditions. On top of which, she'd slapped his face hard, when he'd come on to her at Daniel's birthday party last week; he couldn't allow her to get away with it.*

Seating himself at the bar, Henry glanced through the windows, relishing Bobby's white face. Then Dan was there, putting his arm around her and leading her down the steps, away from the Mess. *The Regimental Second in Command's son really ought to have better taste in women*, thought Henry. True, he'd tried it on with Bobby himself, but he hadn't actually fancied her skinny freckled body and carroty hair. He'd been feeling rather horny that night and one female was as good as another in the dark. Turning back to the bar, he called out, "the cokes are on me everyone." No one took him up on his offer. He turned around to find that he had been talking to an empty room. It didn't worry him – they would be back, he was sure – especially if a whisper began to circulate that the new

Commanding Officer's son was being given a hard time by the other regimental kids.

The Officers' Mess Blenheim Barracks, Salisbury – Summer 2011

"So, does anyone know Dan's replacement?" asked Captain Henry Tennant, helping himself liberally to toast and tea from the trolley, before lowering his elegant frame into one of the deep leather armchairs scattered around the Mess anteroom. From behind a copy of '*The Times*,' the gruff Scottish voice of the Station Staff Officer, Colonel Kenneth Macdonald, gave Henry the answer he was looking for. "A damned fine young officer is joining us…same intake as my son James. Won the sword of honour. Search and Rescue pilot with the Army Air Corps. Done four tours in Iraq. We're lucky to…"

"My, my! A positive paragon," Henry's bored drawl cut in. "Why is such a high flyer joining our humble Rifles here in Salisbury, when he's done such exciting stuff? Slumming it a bit, ain't he?"

The pages of the newspaper rustled in disapproval. The retired colonel had no time for Captain Tennant. *If I was still on the Active List, I would take great pleasure in putting a stop to his shenanigans and make the young idiot do his job! He was able enough when he put his mind to it. The trouble was, he was doing his accepted stint in the military before joining his family's merchant bank. Consequently, he was just coasting along with no incentive to excel, content to let his warrant officers and sergeants do all the work. It was time someone whipped him into shape or threw him out of the army.*

"Gaining all arms experience before going to Staff College." Major Daniel Garrett strolled through the door. He dropped a bulging rucksack on the floor and poured himself a cup of tea.

"Oh Lord! Save me from my earnest career-minded peers! Why can't you all lighten-up – relax and play the game," sighed Henry.

"Because it isn't a bloody game! Lives are at stake. Make a wrong decision and men and women die! You can play and still get promoted because your uncle is on the General Staff – no CO is going to ruin his own career prospects by telling him that his nephew is an arse," an anonymous voice muttered.

Henry ignored the rude comment – there were always those who envied his connections. Why should he wear himself out trying to gain promotion when there was no need?

"Ah…you've seen the promotion list then," he chuckled. "I put up my crowns in January and, unlike some, I didn't run myself ragged in order to get noticed…everything comes to he who waits," he added looking directly at Dan.

"Nepotism is alive and well amongst the Generals," snorted another voice.

Daniel shook his head at his Second-in-Command. "Major Tennant, God help you, or more importantly your new Company – when you go to Afghanistan in the New Year!"

Henry rose languidly to his feet and bowed mockingly. "I shall contrive, my friend. I always do." Laughing, he sauntered out into the hallway and up to his room.

Poor Dan, he mused. *He takes life far too seriously and is so easy to bait…he is also a right pain in the neck – always checking up on me. Still, he'll be out of my hair tomorrow, off to do Commando training…and life is going to be a lot easier for the next few months with no Dan around. I'll be able to run rings around the new guy, who'll know bugger-all about running a Rifle Company.*

The next morning, Henry breezed into the company office with a ready excuse for tardiness on his lips, but stopped dead at the sight of a slim figure at the window, overlooking the parade square. *Well this is a bit of a surprise*, he thought. *Dan's stand-in is a woman!* He was swift to see the advantages of the situation; he mentally rubbed his hands in satisfaction. With a bit of flattery and sweet-talking, he'd have her eating out of his hand in no time. Women rarely resisted him when he put on the Tennant charm.

With a smile and a hand outstretched he moved closer, then paused, there was something vaguely familiar about her. He noted a delicate face, and a pair of golden eyes surrounded by dense black lashes. *She was really quite delicious.* He chuckled inwardly; *things were really looking up. He was going to have a fine time until he was deployed in January.*

"Captain Tennant," she began in a husky voice. "Let me introduce myself, Major Roberta Harrison." Henry gaped at her in utter astonishment. The last he'd heard of her was that she'd taken a double first at Oxford – no one mentioned her joining the army to him. His heart sank.

Bloody Hell! The RSM's skinny daughter has metamorphized into this gorgeous female who, unfortunately, was now his boss!

Bobby looked at his shocked face in amusement. "Military rule has it that one salutes when reporting to a senior officer," she observed with an ironic smile. "And we both know what a stickler for rules you are, Captain."

Henry was momentarily at a loss before his supreme confidence reasserted itself. He'd never failed with a woman yet…he was going to have a fascinating time turning this particular saint into a sinner.

Kathleen Swann

Kathleen spent her childhood in rural Cumbria and now lives in North Yorkshire. She enjoyed 26 years of working life in the NHS and now, since her retirement, is spending time studying and writing poetry. Her poems embrace relationships with family and friends and reflects a love of rural life and its characters. Kathleen takes us with her on visits to other countries and cultures as she observes human behaviour. Her poems are published online, in anthologies, magazines and brought together in her first collection 'Ripples beyond the Pool'. In 2019 Kathleen worked with a young composer to produce a song which was performed at the International Leeds Lieder Festival.

Adrift

We never said goodbye
my mother and I
we travel in the ambulance
holding hands   making plans
talk of tomorrow
we both know this is not
the way it will be
I listen to calm voices
of paramedics   reassuring
and I look out of the window
at grey light and bare trees
the very depth of winter.

The hospital bed is too big
the bedclothes too flimsy
I slide my hand under the sheet
so your warm fingers
as light as a bird's wing
can rest untroubled in mine
I tell you the things we are doing
the bustle of our lives
whilst you lie silent   undecided
your breath is light as thistledown
slow as dreams
and I am adrift.

City Dwellers

marmalade and black cat
hunt with the rat pack
footprints in the snow cat
sneaking down the alley

catching mice and rats cat
trotting on the wall cat
landing on the dustbin
a 'steel-band' playing tabby

house cat or wild cat
living off their wits cat
purr at city fat-cats
licking up the cream

filing down his claws cat
to hang out with the cool cats
tripping down the bus track
street lights make him mean

siamese la-di-da cat
scoffs at raggy pole cat
scrapping with a persian
caterwaul resounds

singing with the tomcats
sniffing out a queen cat
slinking back at dawn cat
the milkman's on his rounds

Song of the Tide on Walney Island

Sing of the dunlins
disguised in the shingle
riffling and prodding
their beaks in the sand
    the grey seals swimming
on the rill of water
bobbing their heads
above waves in the wind.

Sing of the cattle
whose inherent instinct
brings them to safety
to graze on salt grass
    white-crossed oystercatchers
lined up in regiment
stabbing for food
backs to the tide.

Sing of the hills
rising in sunshine
look down on the town
the factories below
    windswept flowers
sea holly   horned poppy
 sealed to the seashore
 by salt-spit wind.

Corvus Girl

She is crow
wraithlike shape perched
on rough black rocks
calling to the sky with dry parched voice
windswept ragged coat unraveling
shreds peeling into air
swirl into feathers
form wings
lift her to sky
fly
away

Piel Island in the Wind

There drifts a castle in the mist
        by the shore   in the sea
                in the rain
a ragged shell calling
            to seals   to waves
    to sea birds
                across incoming tide

raindrops prattle in my ear
        as white-crossed
                oystercatchers   drift
        to land in the midst of the flock
screech   fret   wait
            beaks to the wind

rising tide fills rills and channels
            scatters waders
        to run   search
            dip beaks
                in wakening mud
            shellfish move and open

eider swim in strict formation
            young ones trail
                in deepening water
            greenshanks scurry
            bow and jostle
        racing gulls in rising tide
all drawn to a castle in the mist

Wide-Eyed

The gathering crowd hesitate   anticipate
encouragement needed
to turn their heads his way

Forty minutes to sell his pitch
make his mark   earn his stars
on a teeming street in Edinburgh

He weighs the mood   spills words
pounces
            proffers danger
                        breathes excitement
his life on the line for them

In no time he's up the ladder
balanced astride the top rung
rides the cobbles to stay upright

He sheds his tee shirt   then his kilt
casts aside his   inhibitions
lost to the clapping of the crowd

I watch your face   you're mesmerised
fearful for his safety   unsure of the reaction
when he calls for   three sabres

the ladder walking
            sabre juggling
                        hand clapping
all become one and you
        you are hooked   smitten
engulfed   by   festival fever

Turpentine & Beeswax

Tall frame bent over the bench
the tip of your tongue between your teeth
time meant nothing, dovetails and dowels
were fashioned with care, sharp chisels
shaped gentle curves across the grain
releasing the inner pattern of waves.

Smokey warmth from the iron range
carried the wood's spicy smell
through the oak-beamed rooms
of the old cottage cellar
oak sawn from trees that had
given way to age many years ago.

Outside a wool-white sky lay over hills
filled the wood with shifting mist
hung crystal drops on the cherry tree
as we drank sweetened tea from mugs
placed teacake dough in the bread oven
in memory of my grandmother.

Wood and workbench now long gone
I lift the old tool bag from its rusty hook
carefully wrap each implement
in its own soft cloth, lay them in the bag
the old smell of turpentine and beeswax
turn the dusty air to remembered perfume

Lesley Taylor

Born in rural Hertfordshire, Lesley has lived in London, West Yorkshire, Somerset, Berkshire and North Yorkshire, where she has since remained, living in eight different parts of that large county. 'Moving around this island is a good way to learn to appreciate diversity, both linguistic and cultural. Lesley worked for the public sector for twenty-five years before retiring. Since then, writing for pleasure has become a very enjoyable and rewarding activity.

Roses and grapes

Picture this: a fragrant garden of yellow roses; the sound of water splashing in a stone basin.

An open window above the garden, sends a gentle breeze, neither too cold nor too hot, onto a wide, white-sheeted bed.

The door opens and he is there: her lover. A handsome man, dark-haired, dark-eyed, with smooth brown skin. He smiles and moves towards her in his pure white robe. He has a bunch of pale green grapes in his hand and he sits beside her to share the fruit. In the background music gently plays. As they feed one another the grapes, he runs a fingertip along her arm, the first time he has touched her since last night. She turns towards him and smiles. He has such beautiful eyes, such fine hands. She leans towards him and kisses his cheek. His cool skin smells of soap and spice. They laugh, thinking of last night, of their unstoppable passion, and how slowly and gently they touch each other now. She notices the dark curls on his neck and his long, dark lashes as they sit together, side by side, and he smiles at her, in the rose-scented air, on the wide, white-sheeted bed.

The Busker

I was sipping coffee outside the cafe when I first saw him.
He stood up slowly, tall and thin, wearing a blue woollen scarf and a long
black coat.
Suddenly: a person, not a bundle of old clothes
left lying on the floor.
He stamped his feet to get the blood flowing
then produced a silver flute.
After a few moments, he started to play.
At first softly, before gaining strength:
confidence:
rolling, rollicking, wonderfully complicated
intoxicating musical patterns.
This man was no ordinary busker,
this man was some kind of entrancing magician.

Desert Water

The two of them were tired and suddenly unbearably thirsty and hot, even with the air conditioning roaring. They had taken the Land Rover across at least two hundred miles of sandy, rocky terrain since leaving the little desert town that morning. They were travelling under a punishing, searing sun, and now needed to stop, rest and drink some water.

Martin – driving – tried to find a patch of shade, but there was none. The thin prickly shrubs provided nothing but a scribble of shadow: heat from the sandy ground reflected back at them like the blast from a hot oven. There was absolutely no relief. They stopped and Martin climbed out, opening the boot.

"Jeez!" He yelled, "the water's not here! Only the damned petrol."

He himself had watched the boy load the bottles, before going to check the engine oil and tyres. He had left the vehicle for about five minutes to collect some bags, and the water must have been taken then. That was the only explanation: someone must have stolen it.

Ahead lay a further two hundred miles without anything to drink and already, they were feeling lightheaded. Going back was as hopeless as continuing.

Now Ben drove, struggling to concentrate on the featureless terrain for lack of water and the difficulty of keeping to the ill-defined, sand strewn road. From time to time he thought he saw something in the distance, but the heat was disorientating.

A small dark object lay on the ground ahead. A rock or a mirage?

Closer, they saw it was a large jerry can. Probably empty, or more likely, containing fuel. Ben stopped, walked over to it and unscrewed the cap. The pungent fumes of petrol. Then he looked up and, unbelievably, a line of three camels appeared. Advancing slowly, sedately, swaying as they came, with two men – robed in white – seated on their backs. These desert-dwelling men would have water. These men would surely help them.

He waved and one of the figures waved back. But even as he watched, the camels began turning aside, beginning to follow a diagonal path away from them.

Ben yelled out, his voice cracked and dry. "Help," he shouted. "Help us. *Au secours*."

The little caravan of camels stopped. The seated figures turned to look at them.

Ben began walking towards them, stumbling over loose sand, taking several minutes to reach them. Martin watched. Ben knew some French and possibly the Bedouin would understand him. He began gesturing, explaining as best he could what had happened. Then Martin heard laughter. One of the camel men was laughing and shaking his head.

Ben was then given a flask and was drinking.

The men slowly turned their animals towards the vehicle and Ben followed, staggering a little in the heat. The camel drivers put a simple sort of awning up next to the Land Rover, and immediately created a pool of shade. The animals folded themselves down nearby, eyes closed.

The Bedouin spoke little but shared some water, and some dates. One of them said quite clearly and unexpectedly, "You are English?"

"No. Australian."

The two Bedouin exchanged some words and then nodded and smiled.

"My father say you very lucky. We like Australian. But you are mad. No water very bad problem." He passed them a big leather flask and refused an offer of money. Then after twenty minutes, as quietly as they arrived, they packed up their awning, climbed onto their animals and went on their way, with a smile and a wave.

Before long, they were out of sight. The water in the flask was warm and smelled strong, like drinking from old leather boots, but it was the most wonderful taste. Reviving, life-giving – essential.

As they drove West, towards their destination, Martin and Ben considered how amazing it was that they had met the Bedouin at that exact moment, when they could so easily have missed them. They had seen no one else at all, not another soul, for miles.

They thought about the crystal clear, cold, bottled water at the hotel, and compared it with the warm liquid in the animal skin pouch. First world: third world. They each took a drink from the leather flask, nodded and drove on; both silent, thoughtful and utterly thankful.

Georgie Goes Missing

"Ok, we're home," Emma said, catching her son's eye in the rear-view mirror.

"Goodie" he smiled and began unfastening his seat belt. He didn't like shopping and was glad to be back.

"I need your help with the groceries, please, love."

She had parked by the side gate and let him out of the car. The vehicle was full of the week's shopping – and she selected a bag and handed it to Georgie: one which was not too heavy for a four-year-old to carry. They began to take the first lot of shopping into the garden and up to the house door.

"It's going to be hot today," Emma said, "Maybe later we can sit in the shade with an ice cream."

"Ooh yummy." Georgie jumped up and down. He asked for a glass of water, gazing up at her as he drank.

They then went back to the car for the next lot of bags and boxes.

The neighbourhood was quiet but that was not unusual in this small Napa Valley town, in the middle of a weekday morning. Emma put the food in the various compartments of the huge American fridge freezer – then went back to the car for the remainder of the groceries.

Georgie was now playing under a tree on his yellow trike. "Hey, you need some sun cream on your arms and legs," she called.

About five minutes later, she came out again with the sun cream. "Georgie! Where are you?" There was no sign of him, so she walked round to the rear yard to see if he was there. The front gate was open. The gate which was usually secured with a safety catch to keep him in the garden. "Oh God. Georgie!"

She ran out into the street, looking in both directions but could not see any sign of him. The road ended to one side of their house with a solid fence and a hedge, beyond which was the highway. In one direction, there was a narrow footpath between the fence and some back gardens, – which led towards the little town centre.

In the other direction, the street went gently downhill to a crossroads and then further down to a busy road, where the school was, (and where Georgie's elder brother would now be). There was no one about and certainly no sign of her younger son on his yellow tricycle. Emma felt a lurch of panic.

Which direction to begin to look for him?

She ran to the narrow footpath and called his name. The path was empty, but curved after about fifty yards. Perhaps he had gone further along out of sight?

She ran to the bend and called "Georgie!" again, but he wasn't there. She hurried back to the house and on towards the first crossing. Before she got to the junction a car came along and her heart banged in her chest. "Oh Georgie, wherever are you?"

Frantic with worry and fear and not knowing what to do she ran home, grabbed her bag from the kitchen table and began running again down the road and down the hill. Cars occasionally passed, but no one was walking. At the next crossing, she stopped and looked around, calling out his name.

A man was working in a garden, but shook his head when she asked if he'd seen a small boy on a tricycle.

It was feeling too hot for comfort. Sweat trickled down her back and darkened her tee shirt.

She turned and rushed home, grabbed the car keys and began driving around slowly and carefully, up and along and down the grid of streets. She passed a person walking a dog, who shook his head when she spoke to him. No small boy, no yellow trike.

The car felt cooler with the air conditioning going, calming her a little. He must be nearby somewhere. He must be. He must be.

She turned once more towards the valley bottom, down the street which she had walked that morning with both boys on the way to school. She hoped and prayed that Georgie hadn't gone down there to try and get to the school – on the far side of the busy through road.

She stopped the car, unable to see clearly through her tears. It must be nearly half an hour since she had missed him. She blew her nose and wiped her eyes and rested her head on the steering wheel. When she looked up again, she realised that there were two elderly people standing further down the road talking to a policeman beside a blue car. She could see a small yellow bike.

"Oh no, not an accident. Please, please not an accident."

She moved the car forward and pulled up a few yards from them. She got out and stumbled along towards the group, looking for some sign of Georgie.

"Have you seen my son?" she managed to ask.

They looked at her. Saw she was distressed, and the elderly woman said "Your boy? Is this your boy?"

There he was sitting in the front of the police car eating an apple. He turned and smiled at her. She wanted to go and hold him and hug him, but the policeman was standing in the way.

"We called the officer", the woman said. "He was going along on his bike toward the traffic, no sign of anyone with him. We were worried. We spoke to him. He said his Mom was back at the house."

"Oh, thank you so much, thank you," Emma managed to say.

The policeman took charge. "Please get in the car ma'am," he said.

Emma sat in the blue vehicle with Georgie on her lap.

"Mummy, why is your face wet?" he said.

The next fifteen minutes were not comfortable or easy. She found herself being the subject of some close questions. Why was her child out alone? What kind of parent was she? Didn't she appreciate the danger? Was she fit to be in charge of a child? The officer was tough and serious. She tried to explain what had happened, but he seemed unimpressed and threatened to report her to a social worker. He asked where the house was, what was the address, what her husband did for a living. He made notes in his notebook.

Finally, he said, "OK. Don't ever let something like this happen again." Then, at last, he said she could go, and he sat and watched her as she and Georgie walked up to their car hand in hand.

"Hey!" the officer called out just as she got there. "Your kid's cycle is still here."

She nodded and opened the door and fastened Georgie into his seat. The man came up to her with the tricycle and handed it over, shaking his head. She noticed he had cold, pale-blue eyes.

"You British?" he asked then.

She nodded. He walked back to his vehicle, muttering something as he left.

Emma was wary of Californian policemen – who carried guns and behaved as if everyone was an offender. Her elderly car seemed to them to be an offence in itself, in this rich place. Did she really want her sons to grow up in this unforgiving country? Her husband loved the hot climate and it was indeed, wonderful; could he be persuaded to swap it for chilly old England? Today might be the start of that discussion.

Long green skirts

Wearing lovely, long green skirts,
swishing almost to the ground –
elegantly, they toss their heads
twinned beads in their tresses.
Tall and graceful avenues,
planted by once-important men,
as a gateway to their land –
now a simple village entrance.
Double lines of finest limes
in light green summer dresses.

Old hands

Her hands lie in her lap –
fingers twisted and misshapen
knuckles gnarled and swollen
from arthritis
the blue veins are knotted ropes
of blood vessels growing older
with her day by day
over ninety years
they now lie unmoving
in her sleeping lap captured
like a perfect Rembrandt
or a Leonardo drawing

Old Love

"Love's young dream," Drusilla said, coming back in from the balcony.

"Who?" Jessie asked.

"Young couple walking past, hand in hand. Takes you back."

Druse eased her bulky body into the seat she always used. The smell of cigarette smoke clung to her clothes.

"My Lucy will be sixty-five next week!" Jessie said, writing a message in a birthday card.

"And as for you and me, we'll both be ninety this year!" Drusilla laughed with a smoker's gurgle, like water going down a drain.

In the corner, Frank appeared to be asleep. "You're just kids!" he muttered. Frank would be ninety-five in the Autumn.

"I like to see young folk, with all their lives ahead of them. Like those two out there. What will they live to see?" Jessie wondered, fumbling in her bag for a stamp.

Frank roused himself. "Maybe we've seen the best of it. There's no money for anything now." He had been a firebrand union man in his working days. Both of his veined hands lay outside the blanket which covered his knees. He began waving one arm about. "By God... if I was younger," he said "I'd go into politics. What a lot of idiots they are. All of them. Need their heads banging together."

"Go on Frank," Jessie said, "I like it when you get going. If I was younger I'd be after you....!"

For some reason that stopped Frank in his tracks. He looked at her with his pale eyes – and smiled. For once, Druse said nothing.

Jessie and Frank began spending more time together: he was still able to walk slowly, with two sticks – and she with one. Every afternoon, after they had finished lunch, they made a slow circuit of the sheltered, covered pathway round the Home where they lived. It was level and even, and had a pleasant outlook over a central plant-filled garden. There were some benches where they could stop and rest. If it was raining, they were able to keep dry.

During their walks they talked about one another's lives. She loved to hear about his rousing union days, as a printer for a national newspaper and he listened to her tales of running a home for unmarried mothers. He was a bit deaf, but she spoke clearly, and he heard her well enough. They would often laugh together and other residents called them 'the lovers'.

They would sit side by side in her room and watch television, usually the news and current affairs and she read bits of the daily papers to him. He sometimes held her hand and helped her with the crossword. They both seemed to have found a new lease of life.

The walks led to yoga classes, where they exercised gently and enjoyably.

One morning, Drusilla suggested that Frank and Jessie should get married.

"You think she'd have me?" Frank said, seriously.

Druse thought he should ask her, which was what he did.

Jessie said "That sounds good to me. You're the nicest man I know. Let's have a ceremony on your birthday!" Frank couldn't have been more delighted.

She ordered a cream coloured dress and planned to hold a bunch of pale roses.

He found a dark suit in his wardrobe from twenty years ago, worn once to a grandson's graduation. It still fitted perfectly. He bought, online, some new red socks, and a matching tie with Jessie's help, as she had learned to use a laptop.

He gave her the ruby ring which had been his mother's, and which, by chance, looked good on her. Secretly, other residents clubbed together to buy them a crystal vase which would be filled with flowers on the day and presented to them.

Then the news came which stopped them all in their tracks.

Frank, it turned out, was still married. He and his wife had not been together for years and he had forgotten that they had never got 'round to being divorced. For the past six years, she had suffered from dementia and was now a frail ninety. He was thrown completely by this and didn't know how to face Jessie or the other residents.

When she heard the news, Jessie had looked at Frank for a moment or two, before getting up and going over to him. She saw that his eyes were full of tears. She took her tissue and wiped them dry. Then she put her arms around him and smiled.

"Hey, it doesn't matter," she said. "We'll still have a party on your birthday, and everyone can dress up and celebrate. We'll have a pretend wedding with a broomstick. It will be fun and who cares that it won't be official?".

And that is what happened. They were 'married' on Frank's ninety fifth birthday, with a wedding cake, and music from the sixties, photographs, and a lot of laughter.... and a broomstick to step over. Both were as happy as the young couple that Druse had spotted outside, all those weeks before.

Sue Williams

Since retiring from her day job, Sue has been busy researching her family history and, much to her surprise, has found that although born and bred in Hertfordshire, she has impeccable Yorkshire roots stretching back to the sixteenth century.

Sue has also embarked on writing a biography which covers many of the peace protests of the 1980s and the impact they had on many of the people involved. However, Sue particularly enjoys writing stories with a humorous twist and is also working on a novel about five elderly ladies who get up to all sorts of mischief proving that it's not just the young who know how to enjoy themselves.

Molly's Story

Molly stirred another spoonful of sugar into her coffee. The café was quiet and outside the rain was beating against the windows. She knew she should be in school and it was only a matter of time before someone from the home came looking for her, but she was past caring. There would be the endless discussions, plans, contracts of good behaviour… Ways to make her conform. Not that they weren't nice enough and her key worker Fay was very kind but who wants to live in a home? Still, where was home? Her mother a smack head who would do anything to get the next fix, and her beloved sister gone. Her grandparents said they couldn't cope with her and the foster carers said that she was too disruptive. Well, who wouldn't be with her family? She scowled at her coffee and stirred it viciously.

"Hey, what's that coffee ever done to you?" Molly suddenly became aware that the boy at the next table was watching her intently. He smiled warmly at her and she hesitantly smiled back.

"That's better; you're much prettier when you smile."

"I was thinking," said Molly haughtily.

"Not happy thoughts. I'm Dan in case you want to know, and I was wondering what a pretty girl like you was doing in here."

"Isn't it obvious?" She replied. "I should be in school and I'll get a right bollocking when I'm missed."

"I can give you a lift. Then they may not have realised that you weren't in."

"Do you have a car?"

"It's an old Beamer but I'm waiting for my new one to be delivered. Do you fancy a ride?"

Molly studied Dan thoughtfully. With brown hair and brown eyes, he wasn't exactly good looking but there was something about him, some kind of charm. He wasn't from around here that was for sure. Suddenly she got up and made for the door.

"Okay, you can take me, it's the High School."

Outside Dan opened the car door for her. She slid onto the leather seat and waited for him to get in.

"I've got some business in the area this afternoon, do you want me to come and pick you up from school?" Molly looked at him suspiciously. He was older than her, maybe 19 or 20 and she wasn't so naïve to think that he wasn't after something… But then it would be one over her friend Laura who was always boasting about her different boyfriends.

"If you like," she muttered, "I'll be out at 3.30."

And that was how it all began. Dan frequently seemed to have business to attend to near Molly's school and his old red car was often to be seen waiting for her. He was kind and considerate and so different from the boys she had known before with their impatient and awkward fumblings. He treated her with respect, and they had been meeting for two weeks before he even kissed her.

"You're special Moll, and I don't want to do anything you don't want."

He took her to dimly lit clubs where the doormen all knew him and they drank luridly coloured cocktails which made Molly giggle and her head spin. Then there were the gifts, the clothes that she wore just for him, the short skirts and low cut tops which somehow softened her and made her look more like a young woman than the angry girl in the harsh jeans and tee shirts that she usually wore. He even bought her a new mobile so that she could contact him at any time. He took her old phone off her and threw it away. Molly began to protest because it still had her sister's old mobile number in it, but then, she thought, it doesn't matter anymore. Let it go.

And he made love to her. She'd had sex before with the boys at the home, teasing them, but despising them in their pathetic attempts to please her. This was different. She wanted Dan, wanted him in a way she had never wanted anybody or anything before. She ached for him and then turned away from him because it all seemed too much. He brought her jewellery, a gold chain and a ring and told her she was special. When she was sixteen, they would move in together and he would take care of her forever.

Would this last forever? Dan was very careful. He would drop her off just 'round the corner from the home, so the staff wouldn't see him and ask questions. He said that she had to go to school because they would be after her if she bunked off and he didn't want her getting into trouble. Yet, already people had noticed that she was different, she didn't hang round with the other girls after school anymore and she spent all her free time with Dan. They would go to his flat where they had sex; afterwards he would take her back to the home as he always had business to attend to late at night. She asked if she could go with him but he said that she was too young and that business was for grownups. Then she would get mad and they would end up fighting. She would threaten to leave him but he would just laugh. He knew that without him she had nothing, just the home and the endless, dreary routine of waiting for something, anything, to happen.

* * *

When did it start to go wrong? Dan started to take Molly out more, to different clubs where young women entertained in private booths. He introduced her to some of his friends who came to his flat and they teased her as she sat quietly in the corner. They would drink beer and make remarks about her hair, her makeup and her body. Dan became more distant and began to get impatient with her, criticising her if she wasn't nice to his friends. Then came the dreadful day when she argued back and Dan hit her. Molly was stunned. She knew all about violence, her mother's assorted boyfriends had made sure of that but she hadn't seen it coming with

Dan. Were all men like that? Was it her fault? Had she provoked him? Dan said nothing.

* * *

She didn't see him for a few days after that. She looked for him in all his old haunts, but he seemed to disappear and then, when she had almost given him up, he called her and arranged to meet again. It was as if nothing had happened, he took her back to the flat, they had sex and he gave her a gold bracelet, but afterwards, he was very quiet and withdrawn.

"Is everything okay Dan?" Molly enquired anxiously.

He hesitated for a moment. "I'm in trouble, deep, deep trouble. Do you remember Al?" Molly nodded.

"We did some business and now I owe him a lot of money and he is threatening that if I don't pay up soon, he'll be after me. He's vicious Moll and I'm worried, seriously worried."

"Can't you go to the Police?"

"What will they do? Al will laugh it off and say it was only a joke but I've seen what he does to people who get on the wrong side of him."

"Is there anything I can do?"

Dan looked at her carefully.

"Well, yes, no. I can't ask you. It wouldn't be right."

"What?" Molly almost screamed.

"He'll write off my debts if you agree to sleep with him."

* * *

Molly sat in bed. She wore her old tee-shirt, hugging the duvet to her chest. Outside the bedroom door Dan was waiting for Al to arrive, he was due in five minutes. There was a loud knocking on the door.

"Open up, it's the Police."

Dan made for the window. The door of the flat burst open, there was shouting and screaming as the police burst in and wrestled Dan to the floor. Molly slowly got off the bed and went through to the living room. She looked at Dan and then at the two police officers who were holding him.

"I was beginning to get worried that you wouldn't make it in time and I would have to sleep with Al," she said.

"Moll, what's happening? What have you done to me?" Dan was pale and shaking, his face a mixture of anger and bewilderment as he was led away.

"I'll tell you what's happening," Molly snapped. "Do you remember Emmy Scott? She was my sister and she killed herself because of what you did to her. You're scum, you're less than scum and I hope you rot in hell but at least you won't be pimping any more girls for a long time."

"It's okay Molly, it's over, you've done brilliantly."

Molly noticed that one of the police officers had remained behind. Silently, Molly pulled off the microphone and wire from under her tee shirt and passed it to her.

"I promised Emmy that I'd get him. Before she died, she told me what he had done and I said I would make him pay. He never suspected. I loved my sister, she looked after me and he took her away from me. He killed her, he killed her…."

* * *

Molly stirred another spoonful of sugar into her coffee. The café was quiet and the rain was beating against the windows. She knew she should be in school. A young man was sitting at the next table. He smiled at her. She didn't smile back.

True Lust

"Get yourself to Amsterdam" they said, "the hottest girls in town and they'll do anything you ask for," they said. I had been in London for a few weeks on business and the natives hadn't exactly been friendly. The guys in the office were pleasant enough but they disappeared off to the suburbs in the evenings and London is a lonely city at night on your own.

I was due a few days' leave, so I caught an early flight to Amsterdam. It was a pretty city with old houses and canals but that wasn't why I was there. The red-light district was easy to find. Why, they even put signs pointing the way. I wandered the streets gazing at the semi-naked girls who waved and smiled at me from their windows. They were hot but I wasn't sure. It all felt too much, and I thought of what my Sunday school teacher would have said about this. But then I remembered her soft skin and gentle touch as she tried to explain some obscure bit of the bible to me. In truth she wasn't much older than me and I spent many a Sunday in church dreaming of how I could get her to indulge in at least one of the deadly sins.

My resolve stiffened as I wandered up and down the streets gazing at temptation. Still I hesitated and then I saw the one. Plump, luscious with soft, billowing contours and a come-hither look. For ten long minutes, I stared at the window. This was way beyond the dreams of a spotty schoolboy from Saskatchewan. I had never seen anything like it. I wanted to feel her, stroke her and bury my face in her voluptuous folds. I wanted to lick her, bite her, smother her in kisses...

Let's be honest, she wasn't cheap but quality never is. My heart was pounding, I was shaking with excitement. I took a deep breath and walked through the door. 'I'll have that one' I said to the woman in charge. She smiled knowingly and picking up her tongs, carefully put the biggest, creamiest chocolate cake I had ever seen, into a bag.

Putting the Record Straight – a story about the Brontes

Dear Mrs Gaskell,

What a sad loss dear Charlotte is to her friends and the world, but I am delighted that you are writing her biography. I didn't know Charlotte very well, but I thought you may be interested in my own modest recollections of the family particularly about Emily and her stories.

The trouble with Emily Bronte was that she was always talking to the servants. I can picture her now, snug by the fire with that old tabby Ellen Dean, listening to her gossip and taking it all in. Mrs Dean was one of old Mr Bronte's parishioners and Emily thought very highly of her, so much so that she wrote down all her stories and managed to get them published as Wuthering Heights. Absolute rot, Windy Heights was good enough for Mr Earnshaw but not dramatic enough for our Emily. Too much imagination that girl had and now everyone thinks of moor folk as seething with unbridled lust and passion, rather than the sensible, sober Yorkshiremen and women we really are.

Let me tell you what really happened. Mr Earnshaw was a good man and when he brought Heathcliff home, it was with no more thought than if he had adopted a stray mongrel. He thought he was doing a kindness, but Heathcliff didn't want to be rescued. He came from the slums of a large noisy city and the house even with Cathy, was very quiet and remote. Small wonder he was always in mischief, he was bored. As for Catherine, well she was always wild and wilful. Mrs Dean was very fond of her, having no children of her own and she offered to teach Catherine to bake the cakes and delicacies she was so fond of. "Oh no," said Madam, "when I get married, it will be to a rich man with plenty of servants, so I won't need to know how to cook." Heathcliff couldn't say he hadn't been warned but he had nothing to offer her, being no more than a poor charity case dependent on the goodwill of his master. Catherine may have been devoted to him, but she would have no more married a pauper than she would have given up all the little fripperies she was so fond of.

However, when Heathcliff came back to Yorkshire, he was a wealthy man having been employed by Jacob Ollershaw who was one of old Mr Earnshaw's business partners. Mr Ollershaw had made a great deal of money from the Lancashire coal fields and when he sadly passed away, he left his property and business interests to Heathcliff whom he had come to look on as a son.

Of course, it was too late for Catherine as she was already married to Edgar Linton and expecting their first child. Many a young girl was ready to take her place, but Heathcliff would have none of them. He stormed, he wept, he cursed the perfidy of the sex (I apologise dear Mrs Gaskell for my intemperate language but I don't want you to think harshly of poor Heathcliff as he suffered terribly and he had been very badly treated by Catherine) and forswore the company of women forever. Like many a man disappointed in love before and since, he threw himself into work and vowed to remain a bachelor forever.

Much has been written about Heathcliff and his harsh treatment of Isabella and Hindley. Of course, Emily had a very vivid imagination and she was very fond of gothic novels with their cruel heroes and panting heroines so nothing would do but for Heathcliff's name to be blackened and he was cast as a most unnatural fiend. This was most unfair. As a young man he always spoke very fondly of Mr Earnshaw and his kindness to him, and although Hindley had been very cruel to him, he treated all Mr Earnshaw's family with the utmost respect. When Heathcliff returned to the Heights, he had tried to reason with Hindley and turn him away from his deadly path of vice and corruption, but Hindley would not listen to anyone. He was already gambling wildly and drinking heavily long before Heathcliff's return and died a miserable, drunkard's death.

As for Isabella, what did she expect? She would not leave Heathcliff alone and pursued him in such a bold and unladylike manner, that he was like a trapped animal. And yet, what did the silly girl do once she had married him? Wept and wailed that life at Wuthering Heights with her new husband was harsh and cruel. I hope I am a good Christian woman and one must not speak ill of the dead, but had she fulfilled her feminine duties and made a warm, cosy home for Heathcliff, her marriage would have been the making of her. Men, as we know Mrs Gaskell, are such simple creatures that if we give them the quiet domesticity and gentle feminine companionship which is their due, they are ours to command. Still it has to be acknowledged that Isabella did have to put up with Joseph with his sour face and sanctimonious ways, which would have been a trial for any young woman. Joseph has long since gone to meet his maker and I just hope that his maker is able to live up to Joseph's exacting standards.

Perhaps Heathcliff's greatest disappointment was his son Linton. He knew nothing about the boy until Isabella's untimely demise, but it has to be admitted that Heathcliff found Linton a sad trial. The boy had all the snivelling, vexatious faults of the invalid and was a most demanding child. Heathcliff by contrast enjoyed the rudest health and, in his youth, so I'm told, was a splendid example of manhood. He tried to be a good parent, but Linton seemed determined to thwart him at every turn. If Heathcliff wanted to go out, Linton was too ill. If Heathcliff said to stay home, Linton moped and said he needed fresh air and exercise. It was not a happy relationship and although Heathcliff mourned Linton's passing, it was tempered with a guilty relief. He then had to deal with young Catherine who had inveigled her way into the little household. She was every bit as wilful as her mother and plagued Heathcliff nearly as much. Moreover, as a very young widow, it was hardly decent that she should be living alone in a house with just Heathcliff and Hareton for company. I do not count the servants of course. The inevitable happened and before she had even moved into half mourning, she had Hareton firmly in her grasp.

Hareton and Cathy did marry but sold the Grange and moved to York where they took their place in polite society. Stories of Heathcliff's demise were circulating wildly at the time when they left but the truth was both more sober and more tragic. His obsession with Catherine Earnshaw had pushed him to the edge of madness and by his own admission; he was a most piteous wretch. He suffered a complete collapse, no doubt brought on by wandering over the moors without proper flannels. The weather up here can be very treacherous, and woe betide the unwary traveller who does not venture forth with a stout pair of boots and a warm muffler. But I digress and must continue with my tale. Heathcliff was taken secretly to the great asylum at York where he was eventually nursed back to health. To his credit, Hareton visited him regularly and after five long years, Heathcliff returned to Wuthering Heights to live in quiet solitude. He resides there to this day, now an old, old man but he is cheerful and content and ready to meet the Lord when his time comes.

And how do I know all this you ask? Well to borrow dear Charlotte's own phrase, "Reader, I married him." Heathcliff had always suffered from bouts of melancholy, but it was nothing that a good, plain-speaking Yorkshire woman couldn't cure. Besides, at twenty-seven I had been on the shelf for far too many years and I decided to take fate into my own hands. When I proposed to Heathcliff, he was so stunned and delighted that he said yes immediately, and I got him to the church before he had time to change his mind.

There are no ghosts here Mrs Gaskell. We were blessed with eight lively children and the only wild wails in this house were when they used to plague the life out of their dear papa who could refuse them nothing. Now it is our grandchildren who are Heathcliff's delight and it does my heart good to see him surrounded by their merry little faces.

I hope my little story is of interest to you and gives you a truer picture of life here at Windy Heights. I am a great admirer of your books and I look forward to reading your life of dear Charlotte and the rest of the Bronte family.

With my very warmest wishes

Your obedient servant

Amelia Heathcliff.

Return to Pemberley

Wuthering Heights
Haworth Moor
Yorkshire

Dear Mrs Gaskell,

Heathcliff and I have been amazed and delighted by your kind and generous response to our little tale of life at Wuthering Heights and it was very kind of you to share it among your friends. I am emboldened to share another little story with you concerning my late uncle Charles Augustus Braithwaite Esquire, otherwise known to all as Uncle Charlie Braithwaite.

My grandmother was blessed with six children and Uncle Charlie was her fourth son and favourite child. The family estate was settled on Uncle George who was the eldest son and it was decided that as Uncle Charlie would have only a modest inheritance, he was destined for the church and a bishopric at least. Unfortunately, as a lowly curate he was found disrobing in the vestry with the vicar's wife, which brought his clerical career to an abrupt end.

There were distant cousins who owned sugar plantations in the West Indies, and it was decided to despatch Uncle Charlie there so he could make a living as befitting a gentleman. By all accounts, Uncle Charlie was very successful and made a substantial fortune but once again he succumbed to animal lusts and left the islands in a hurry after being discovered in an indelicate position with the Governor's wife.

He returned home bronzed, healthy and as irrepressible as ever. By this time his reputation was such that his neighbours kept their wives and daughters well away from him and he amused himself by dallying with our maids and the local farmers' wives. My grandfather became so incensed by his licentious behaviour that he banished Uncle Charlie from the family home, much to the distress of my grandmother. Now Uncle Charlie was very kind-hearted and seeing how upset his mother was, vowed to forsake his wicked ways and become a reformed character. He took himself off to Derbyshire where he purchased a very pretty little estate, adjoining the great house and park of Pemberley.

By this time Uncle Charlie was all of five and thirty, a pleasant looking man with light brown hair and regular features but with a roguish twinkle in his eyes, which had led to the downfall of many a maiden. Yet to everyone's surprise, he happily settled down to the life of a country gentleman, inspecting his farms and getting to know his tenants. He hadn't at that time met his illustrious neighbours but wrote enthusiastic letters to his mama, extolling the virtues of his new life. It wasn't until his beloved mother and his sister Jane descended on him for a protracted stay that he finally met the inhabitants of Pemberley.

The Braithwaite family were invited to dine with Mr and Mrs Darcy and from a polite acquaintance, there soon developed a close friendship amongst the ladies with regular visits between the two houses. Uncle Charlie was to be found hunting and shooting in the company of Mr Darcy and all the Braithwaites declared themselves charmed and gratified by the attention paid to them by their new friends.

Georgiana Darcy was often in the company of her sister in law and although Mrs Darcy chaperoned her very closely, she soon made the acquaintance of Uncle Charlie who for the first time in his life, fell deeply in love. Whether it was Georgiana's quiet demeanour and puppy brown eyes, her devotion to her brother and his wife or her generous marriage portion it was hard to say but there was no doubt that Uncle Charlie was truly smitten. Miss Darcy was equally enamoured with him. Since her disastrous liaison with the unspeakable Wickham, she had lived very quietly at Pemberley and had been very carefully shielded from any male attention. Uncle Charlie erupted into her life like a volcano. He offered her excitement, her own home and an escape from her comfortable but dull life.

Impetuous as ever, it was not long before Uncle Charlie proposed and was eagerly accepted by his blushing bride to be. Contrary to expectations, Mr Darcy raised no objections to the proposed nuptials of his beloved sister. He liked Uncle Charlie and knew nothing to his discredit; tales of Uncle Charlie's previous indiscretions hadn't reached as far as Derbyshire and his mother and sister said nothing, fervently praying that he had truly reformed. Moreover, his fortune although not as magnificent as Mr Darcy's, was respectable enough and would keep Georgiana in the state to which she was accustomed. In fairness to Georgiana, she would have lived in a hovel with Uncle Charlie if that was all he could offer her. She didn't actually know what a hovel was but was convinced it must be a small, rustic dwelling with only enough space for a couple of servants.

No, the only objection came from the most unexpected quarter. Mrs Darcy, the former Lizzy Bennet who had the most vulgar and silliest mother in Christendom and who was the sister-in-law of the odious Wickham, had the temerity to argue that Uncle Charlie wasn't good enough for her beloved Georgiana. She raged, she stormed; she even had the effrontery to summon Lady Catherine de Bourgh to Pemberley to try and make Georgiana see sense. Lady Catherine, never one to shirk her duty, duly arrived in Derbyshire with her daughter Anne, Mr Collins and his wife Charlotte in tow, ready to do battle.

The visit did not go well. Mr Collins was as sanctimonious and pompous as ever, lecturing Georgiana on the errors of her ways and Lady Catherine was not quiet on the subject either. She forcibly reminded Georgiana of her elevated rank and pointed out that Uncle Charlie although undoubtedly a gentleman came from an obscure Yorkshire family and was hardly a fitting suitor. Georgiana ignored them all. She was in love and spent most of her time with Uncle Charlie planning their future together. No, the person who suffered most was Mr Darcy who although he tried to ignore his unwelcome guests, couldn't escape their attentions.

"Fitzwilliam, I'm sure the estate would be so much better if you had an extra gamekeeper just like the one I have at Rosings," Lady

Catherine would inform him kindly "and do you think *eau de nil* is quite the right colour for my bedroom?"

It appeared that the visitors intended to stay at Pemberley for a prolonged visit, but rescue came from an unlikely source. It was Miss de Bourgh who caused the abrupt departure of the party from Pemberley. Despite her august lineage Anne de Bourgh was very thin and sickly with neither charm nor wit to recommend her. She was constantly demanding attention which didn't endear her to her hosts and was as hard and sour as an unripe apple. Now it has been mentioned before that Uncle Charlie despite his faults was a warm and generous man and he felt very sorry for Georgiana's lonely and miserable cousin. He talked to her and paid attention to her, shewing her great kindness much in the manner that he talked to his dogs. Regrettably Miss de Bourgh conceived a violent passion for him and convinced herself that it was only a matter of time before he realised he had made a terrible mistake and would abandon Georgiana for her.

This would have passed unnoticed had not Miss de Bourgh tiring of one of Mr Collins' interminable speeches at the dinner table, suddenly declared to the assembled company that when she married Uncle Charlie, she would no longer have to listen to such rubbish. There was a stunned silence. Even Lady Catherine was momentarily quiet and Uncle Charlie was absolutely mortified, having no idea that his actions could be so misconstrued. I'm sorry to say that two of the footmen sniggered at the drama unfolding before them and had the butler seen them, they would have been seeking employment elsewhere. That's the problem with servants. You either spend all your time trying to get them to perform their duties with a modicum of efficiency or else they are so unobtrusive that you forget they are there and they see and hear far more than is good for them. But I digress. The unhappy girl was dragged away from the table by her enraged mama and the whole party left Pemberley at first light the next day.

Mrs Darcy was a defeated woman and reluctantly conceded that Uncle Charlie and Georgiana should be wed before any more deluded maidens threw themselves at his feet.

Happy is the bride who knows herself beloved. Uncle Charlie and Georgiana were married with everyone's good wishes and all due ceremony in the parish church, and as expected lived happily ever after. Just as his mother and sister had hoped, Uncle Charlie settled down and became a devoted husband and father. And if Georgiana ever noticed any children with light brown hair, regular features and twinkly blue eyes running 'round the estate, she was far too sensible to mention it.

My cousin Augustus now resides in Derbyshire together with his wife who comes from a most distinguished family. Her father was an earl no less and they live in great state as befitting a noble-man's daughter and her husband. Who would have thought the Braithwaites would rise to such great heights? Yes, I am fortunate to belong to a truly remarkable family and I could write so many tales about them. Have I mentioned that Jane Eyre was based on my cousin Maria?

With my warmest wishes

I remain, your obedient servant

Amelia Heathcliff.

Second Best

Oh no, not again. I could hear my parents fighting downstairs. Raised voices, my mother pouring out scorn, mocking my father's inability to provide enough money for the family. Dad had been laid off for the winter and money was very tight. The debt collectors must have been round again. I crept back to bed and pulled the covers over my head.

When I came down in the morning, Mum was sitting at the kitchen table, stirring her tea and thoughtfully smoking a cigarette. She caught sight of me and beckoned me over from where I stood behind the door.

"It's all right Janey, everything is fine." Cautiously I sat down next to her, waiting for the next eruption but she started talking almost as if I wasn't there. She started telling me about when she was a young girl and how life hadn't always been so hard. Then she began speaking about her time in Plymouth during the war and her great romance with a young sailor. She spoke about her family, the things she did and even how she met her young man…

Not again, Eileen thought as a thin, piercing wail cut through the night air. Will these raids ever stop? Pausing only to pick up her coat and gas mask, she hurried down the darkened street to the public shelter. As she rushed down the wet stone steps she slipped and collided with a tall fair-haired young man who was entering the shelter in front of her.

"Are you ok?" the young man asked anxiously, "you've had a wee bit of a tumble."

"I'm fine, just a bit shaken up." Eileen eased past him and went inside the shelter. She was noticeably shaking, and the man went to sit beside her.

"You don't seem alright to me."

Eileen swallowed, "Sorry about this. We were bombed out in Manchester and I had to be dug out. It's silly but every time I hear the siren I start to shake." For the first time she looked at the man who had stopped her falling and smiled shyly at him. She noticed that he had kind blue eyes that crinkled at the corners. "I was sent by mother to stay with my aunt and uncle in Plymouth."

"I thought you weren't from around here," the man smiled encouragingly.

"With an accent like that, neither are you." Eileen was beginning to feel a little calmer; the knot in her stomach slowly unravelling.

"I'm from the borders, but my ship is here for a couple of weeks." The young man leaned back against the wall of the shelter, took out a silver cigarette case and offered her one. Eileen now took the opportunity to have a proper look at him. She noticed his uniform and the second bright gold ring on his sleeves.

"Have you just been promoted to lieutenant?" Eileen asked. The young man looked at her with deepening interest.

"That's very astute of you. I only got promoted this week and had the extra ring put on today."

"A bit of inside knowledge. I have two brothers in the Royal Navy and my dad was in the last war," she said.

"Well my family have always been farmers, so you have a head start on me."

Eileen smiled broadly. "I'm working in my uncle's office and I help out with my aunt at the WRVS canteen two nights a week but I'm waiting for my papers to join the WRNS. It will be an honour to serve with the Royal Navy."

At that moment, the all clear sounded and people started moving towards the exit. "Good night Lieutenant, thank you for reassuring me and good luck when you go back to sea."

Eileen hurried home but smiled to herself as she walked down the road. Since being dug out from the cellar at her home in Manchester, Eileen had always been terrified by air raids. Her chance encounter with the young lieutenant had made her feel better, and somehow, she felt a bit safer with him around.

*   *   *

It was Eileen's evening for helping at the WRVS canteen, serving teas to a long line of servicemen and women snatching brief respite from the war. As she approached the end of her shift, she was surprised to see the man from the air raid shelter approach the counter and she smiled at him.

"Do you know how many WRVS canteens there are in Plymouth?" He smiled back at her. Eileen was dressed simply in a plain white overall with her long hair caught back in a snood, yet all he was aware of was her heart shaped face and lustrous brown eyes.

"Hello Lieutenant, what are you looking for?"

"My friends call me Davy, Miss."

"Well Davy, what would you like? Tea?"

"Well Miss, tea would be very nice but if you are free tomorrow would you like to come with me for a walk on the Hoe?"

"Thank you, that would be lovely."

*   *   *

The sea sparkled as the sunlight danced on the waves. "Race you to Smeaton Tower!" Eileen cried as she shook her hair loose and raced across the green, Davy stood there momentarily transfixed by the carefree young woman running with the wind blowing in her hair.

"Davy, do you not want to race me?" He laughed and quickly caught up with her.

130

"You shouldn't take on the Royal Navy unless you're quicker than that." He smiled and she shyly took his outstretched hand.

The sun was slowly setting as they walked down towards the Barbican. Eileen had never felt this way about anybody before. She glanced up at him 'Thank you for a wonderful afternoon.' Davy looked down at her. "Is it too soon to ask if you'll be my lass?"

"I will be honoured," Eileen said demurely.

Davy caught her up in his arms and twirled her around as if she was no more than a feather in the wind.

"You have made me so happy."

He then became solemn. "We sail at dawn tomorrow and I don't know when I will be back." At these words Eileen felt a chill go through her. So many brave young men had sailed out of Plymouth never to return, their graves unknown and unmarked at the bottom of the sea. She had known Davy for such a short time yet he was already very precious to her. "God go with you," she whispered "and when you return I shall be waiting here for you."

* * *

The next morning dawned cold and grey; a thin wind whipped round the headland at Devil's Point. Eileen hurried down to join the waiting throng of wives and loved ones. A fine drizzle obscured the view out to sea and then slowly through the mist Davy's ship emerged into the channel heading for the open sea. As the ship passed where Eileen was standing it gave two short blasts on its whistle. Was that her Davy saying goodbye? Eileen pulled her coat around her as the tears slowly rolled down her cheeks. He must come back. Wherever he is going, I'll be waiting here for him.

Mum shook her head wonderingly and looked at the small child who was quietly watching her. "He did come back and we were going to be married. Even though it was wartime, your grandad insisted we had a proper wedding in church with a wedding cake and a fancy

131

reception although where he would get the cake, heavens only knows." She sighed, "but Davy didn't come back the next time. We were told his ship was sunk by a U boat in the Atlantic with the loss of all hands...." Her voice trailed off and she stirred another spoonful of sugar into her cooling tea. "I married your father on the rebound. I'd known him for years and he always wanted to marry me. He was kind and dependable but because he had a deformed leg, he wasn't called up. He could fight though. People could be very unkind; he was called a coward and a conchie because he wasn't in uniform. He would get into vicious arguments and became very bitter and angry. He's not really a violent man but life hasn't always been kind to him." She paused and sipped her tea. "One day my girl, you will meet someone like Davy. Don't ever let them go and never settle for second best."

* * *

She never spoke about Davy again but since that day, I have often thought about my poor Dad, second best and despised by my mother for not being the handsome young man she fell in love with all those years ago. I watched my father slowly wither away under her vitriolic scorn until he became nothing more than a pale ghost haunting the edges of my childhood, yet he loved her until he died. Her bitterness and grief poisoned everything and everyone around her, and my childhood was blighted by her misery and rage. I left home as soon as I was old enough, but the memories remain.

And then as so often when I feel myself sinking into gloom thinking about my mother and the past, the door is flung open and my beloved Georgie bursts into the room. Hair flying and face alight with love and enthusiasm; she hugs me and whirls me around the room. 'Don't just sit there moping' she'll say and she will outline some outrageous plan or idea she has just come up with, which leaves us both helpless with laughter.

My mother taught me that people can't be trusted, that a malign fate can ruin lives both in the past and in the present, but I rejected all that hurt and misery. Love comes in many guises and life has been good to me. I married someone who is generous, loving and kind, who cares for me and makes me happy. Someone who is just like my father.

133

Cosily Confidential

Leonard was such a good man people used to tell me, a good husband and friend. And so he was, hardworking, reliable and kind. Never a birthday forgotten or anniversary missed, a pillar of our church and keen member of his local Rotary. Oh yes, Leonard was all of those things. I can see him still. Grey hair, grey eyes, grey skin, dressed in his favourite beige trousers and blue polo shirt. Yet, if I am being totally honest with you and we are being very honest, aren't we, he was just a teensy bit dull. Life was so predictable. I didn't work as Leonard didn't hold with married women working outside the home and we weren't blessed with children, so I only had him to look after. Home at 5:30 each evening for tea. Leonard thought calling our evening meal supper was pretentious and it wasn't grand enough to be called dinner. A pleasant chat about what he had done at the office and then an evening of television or reading. Happy? I suppose we were until that terrible, terrible day…

We were on holiday staying at a little B & B. Leonard didn't like what he called fancy hotels and he preferred to save money where he could. Not mean exactly but careful, definitely not extravagant. It was a grey, murky day and we were walking along the clifftops. I was thinking about my tea when Leonard suddenly slipped. I can still see his look of surprised horror as he went hurtling down to the rocks below. The rescue services came quickly but sadly it was too late.

At the age of 59, I became if not a merry widow, at least a contented one. Leonard was an accountant and left me very well provided for. I treated myself to expensive hairdos, clothes and a delightful trip to Italy, staying in the best hotels. It was there that I met Patrick.

Ah, Patrick, what can I tell you about him? His hair is thick with just a touch of grey and his green eyes just look deep into my soul. I fell for him in a big way. Sex? Oh my dear, the sex was truly wonderful. I never knew that it was possible to want someone so much. I craved his touch, I would do anything he asked, I would dance naked in the moonlight if that's what he wanted. Actually, I did dance naked in the moonlight but that is quite another story.

And what was his attraction to me? I'm not a fool; I'm fifteen years older than him and although I keep myself in trim, my body sags like a deflated balloon. I've no illusions; it's the money that keeps him by my side. I've bought him a new car, expensive clothes and jewellery. He talks about getting married but that will never happen. We've taken out life insurance on each other and I may at some point put his name on the deeds of my house but there's no rush.

The future? Well who knows what the future may bring. He may get tired of me and want to leave or become too demanding, too greedy. Leonard taught me one thing though; always plan for the unexpected. Another fall from a cliff top may rouse suspicions but there are other ways of getting rid. A cruise would be nice, just the two of us. And the sea is a dangerous place where accidents can happen so quickly. Who would ever suspect?

Patrick's Return

Emily looked up from her writing. Was that a creak? But then Matthew had oiled the hinges of the door only yesterday. She shook her head and went back to her novel, thinking about how to make a convincing end of a particularly annoying character that had become very boring.

As the door started to open slowly, she looked up again. There leaning against the doorpost was a tall, slim man who was looking at her with a mildly pained expression

"You shouldn't have got rid of me," he said slowly. "I didn't deserve what you did to me and the way you left me. I have feelings too."

She looked sternly at him. "Patrick, it was nothing personal but why have you come back? We are finished; there is nothing more to say."

"Finished?" He snapped, "Have you any idea what you did to me? Made me a laughing stock that's what you did. Kill me if you must but not at the hands of an insatiable old widow who decided to change me for some old man with pots of money. If I was meant to die, it should have been heroically in battle or in a duel to avenge a maiden's honour, not pushed over the side of some floating gin palace full of geriatric nymphomaniacs."

"Really Patrick, I don't know what you are getting so worked up about. You know the rules. Once a story is finished, that's it. The characters retire back into the pages, waiting for the next reader. You have no right to come here complaining about your end. Besides I didn't actually kill you off, I just left your widow musing on what she could do to you if your relationship didn't work out.' Emily smiled at him. He was one of her favourite characters with his good looks and charm even if he was somewhat mercenary. 'But tell me more Patrick; obviously the story went on beyond my ending. I'm intrigued."

"Why?" he asked, "you created the murderous old hag and she was hardly going to stop at one death, was she? What Claire wanted, Claire got but she was very clever at it and no-one ever suspected. But now it's my turn to get revenge and as I can't finish off Claire, it has to be you.' He quietly shut the door and stood before her. 'You thought it was just a bit of fun didn't you, something to amuse the readers but you didn't think of what you were doing to me."

He reached out to her and seeing the naked hatred in his eyes, for the first time Emily felt afraid. "You don't mean this, it can't be happening…." She screamed as his hands went 'round her neck. "No, no, I don't want to die…."

"Emily. Emily, calm down. You must have had a bad dream." Matthew was holding her, trying to reassure her. "You were screaming."

"It was Patrick, one of my characters and he was taking his revenge on me. Matthew, it felt so real." She sobbed.

"You're fine now. I'm here." His voice was soft and calming and she clung to him.

"I feel so stupid," she said "but it was absolutely terrifying. Look, I'm still shaking." She tried to laugh and held out her hands but then they heard the door creak again.

There was no-one there.

Curtains Close.

Cue Announcer.

We hope you enjoyed ***A Chorus Of Seven***.

Watch for other books by members of The Scriveners and please leave a review with your favourite bookseller.